XX

TRAIL
OF THE
DANGEROUS
GUN

TRAIL
OF THE
DANGEROUS
GUN

•

LEE MARTIN

AVALON BOOKS
THOMAS BOUREGY AND COMPANY, INC.
401 LAFAYETTE STREET
NEW YORK, NEW YORK 10003

PRINTED IN THE UNITED STATES OF AMERICA
ON ACID-FREE PAPER
BY HADDON CRAFTSMEN, SCRANTON, PENNSYLVANIA

To my beautiful mother who could be the heroine
in any of my books
with her sense of humor, spunk, abiding faith, and love

Chapter One

S hot from the saddle, Cass Darringer had rolled across the green grass until he crashed against a rock. Stunned, he couldn't move his legs and felt his body going numb and cold in the afternoon sun. His stallion had run off at a gallop, and he tried to twist his right hand from under him to reach his six-shooter, but his life was ebbing away as he closed his eyes.

He heard movement, someone coming up the hillside, boots clumping on the rocks and brush. Playing dead, he tried not to cringe as someone kicked him in the ribs, over and over, but his big frame was so numb, he hardly felt it. He had trouble hearing their voices even as one man shouted from below.

"Is he dead?"

"Yeah. But he's wearin' an army shirt."

"He could be a scout. Let's get the devil out of here. Them soldiers could be right behind 'im."

It seemed an eternity before he heard horses riding away, and at last, he was able to roll on his side. He knew he was near the camp. His partner Shorty and

1

the three visitors from the railroad had been waiting for him to return from his hunt.

Cass had been shot on the left side of his skull, his head felt about to explode and his vision had blurred. Another bullet had creased him above the left collar bone right through his buckskin coat, and blood was soaking his double-breasted shirt. He told himself he was only twenty-seven, and that was too young to die.

He struggled with his legs until they moved, and he started crawling south over the hill, grabbing the tall grass and rocks as he pulled himself along, little by little. Life began to return to his body and senses.

Now he was on the crest of the rise, and with blood trickling down his rough face and sweat on his slightly hooked nose, his ice-blue eyes narrowed under dark brows, he tried to see the camp down by the creek.

"I can't believe it," he whispered.

Below among the cottonwoods, the three railroad men who had shared their camp were each dangling from a high limb at the end of a rope. Their horses and Shorty's mule had been shot and were lying in silence on the far side of the creek. The dozen, un-branded mustang mares that he and Shorty had picked up along the Bozeman were missing.

They had been warned that even with Sitting Bull gone to Canada, Montana Territory in 1878 was still deadly because of the vigilantes. Heading west, they had made it past the trail to Virginia City to the south, to no avail.

He crawled some more, so terrified he was gasping for air, and then he saw Shorty, lying in a pool of blood, down by the dwindling campfire. In desperation, Cass struggled to his knees, but when he got to his feet, his brain spun crazily, sending him into sudden darkness.

It seemed forever before he was conscious, and his first scent was of lilacs. He could hear the crackling of a campfire and feel its heat on the left side of his face and body. There were mumbling voices of a lot of men.

He was lying on his back, covered with blankets, and there was a small hand pressing a cold towel to his brow. He wondered if he had died.

"How's he doin', Texas?" a man called.

A woman's voice, close to his ear and soft as cotton, answered. "He's still alive."

Cass opened his eyes slowly. Through a blur, he saw flame red hair gleaming in the firelight and cascading about a face bending over him, a face he couldn't see, framed against the stars in the black sky.

An older man was kneeling at his side. He could see a grey beard and an average size frame in a heavy coat. He closed, then reopened his eyes, but the man was still a blur.

"Son, I'm Joker Rafferty. This here's my niece,

Texas. Her and a fellow named Thatcher own this freight outfit. We're just from Salt Lake and up through Virginia City, where we left off our wagons. Come the rest of the way with what was left on the mules. Looks like vigilantes hanged three men here and beat one to death. An old man who must of been trying to stop them."

"Shorty, my partner."

"Right sorry to hear that. We buried 'em on the hill. Dragged off the dead horses and mule so we could stay until you got better. Wasn't sure you was ever gonna wake up."

"Who done it?"

"Don't know. Saw tracks of maybe ten shod horses, and a dozen unshod ponies, and they all headed west, right toward Lost River. But you'll never track 'em on that trail, not with all the wagon ruts and such. Too well traveled. And they got a good day's head start."

Cass closed his eyes. "I thought I was dead."

"Who are you, anyhow?"

"Cass Darringer."

"One of them gunfighters. Heard you rode with the Red River gang some years back, down in New Mexico Territory. Thought they was all hanged. But you don't look so tough right now. Are you seeing double?"

Cass opened his eyes, blinking. "No, but everything's kind of blurred."

"Then you'll be all right. And don't worry. They

won't be back. Besides, there's twelve of us and Texas. You think you can eat?''

Cass felt himself being lifted against a saddle seat, his head upright and still dazed, but Texas was giving him water. He clung to the canteen. She then brought coffee, and he was able to hold the cup, but, although she made him nervous, he allowed her to feed him some beans until he could hold the plate himself.

His eyes were starting to focus as he gazed down along the creek where a lot of men were bedding down and the mules were staked out near his stallion. Goods were heaped with the pack saddles over near the cottonwoods where ropes still dangled.

Joker squatted at his side. The man was maybe sixty, bald with soft grey eyes and a thin nose, his voice crusty.

''The vigilantes must of thought them three fellas was guilty of something.''

Cass shook his head. ''They made a mistake. They worked for the railroad. One of 'em gave me a callin' card.''

''So that's why their pockets was all picked clean, covering up. With you wearin' that army shirt, they must of left in a hurry, figuring the army was right behind you.''

''My stallion, Ranger. He run off.''

''Don't worry, he came back. We rubbed him down

and got him staked out. So, are you workin' for the army?''

"Not any more. Shorty inherited some land in Oregon. That's where we was headed, to start a horse ranch. We'd picked up a dozen mustang mares on the Bozeman. Never had time to brand 'em, because we'd seen signs of the Sioux all the way to the Yellowstone.''

"Well, no problems around here since the Nez Perce charged on through to Wyomin' last year.''

Texas came back to kneel at his side, and the firelight caught her fine features and a spray of freckles across her slim nose and flushed cheeks. In her early twenties, she had large blue eyes and a dazzling smile, the prettiest woman he had ever seen.

She was wearing a white chemise with frills at the throat, a determined contrast to her heavy wool jacket and some kind of riding skirt.

"You had us worried," she said.

Now he realized his head was bandaged, and it hurt. The wound above his left collarbone had been tended and felt cold. He raised himself higher against the saddle, a bit dizzy but feeling stronger.

"You're lucky you was out huntin'," Joker said.

"Shorty was always complainin' he wanted some venison, but his eye sight wasn't so good with a rifle no more. When we camped, we saw signs of deer crossing the creek and headin' north, and I was fed up with his naggin' and went out to have a look.''

"He saved your life."

With that, Joker got up and went over to his blankets.

Texas put a wet cloth on Cass's forehead. "Everyone's heard of Cass Darringer."

It was a long moment before he answered, but since tears refused to fill his eyes and because he was unable to face his grief, he was compelled to tell her the story, his voice sounding far away.

"I ran off when I was fourteen, and the Red River boys took me in and raised me. They was workin' for a cattleman's association, fightin' rustlers, and then we got in a range war about five years ago. I got all shot up and was left for dead. Shorty found me and put me on the straight and narrow."

"Were you an outlaw?"

"I was gettin' there real fast."

She pressed her hand to his brow which had cooled, but she didn't speak, listening to him as he muttered his anger.

"Now Shorty's gone, and I ain't lettin' 'em get away with this. Where would they take my mustangs?"

Joker, who had knelt at his side, answered for her.

"Only two outfits could swallow 'em up around here, and they're both out of Lost River, due west. The Langdons got the biggest spread. And the Poagues, a bunch of bad apples, they got a place north of town, on the other side of Whiskey Gulch, a canyon nobody's got the guts to enter.''

"One was a pinto mare with a cross on her shoulder. I'll know 'em on sight. Had 'em broke to lead.''

"We get to Lost River, you go see Sheriff Webb and let him take care of it. Nobody likes him much, but he's tough, and he does his job.''

His vision normal, Cass looked around the camp. Four men were on guard, and the others, mostly gruff and bearded, were weary and gulping down their food so they could sleep. Texas had gone over to check the coffee. Her hair glistened in the firelight.

Later that night, Cass lay in his blankets, his head on his saddle and his gaze on the stars, a silent prayer on his lips. And when he could pray no more, his thoughts turned to vengeance. Somebody was going to pay for this.

It was often said in the state of Texas: Never make a Darringer mad. And Cass was as mad as he had ever been.

In the morning, Cass's vision was clear, and he insisted he could ride his stallion, although he was a bit dizzy. They headed west on a wide, muddled path of endless wagon ruts and prints that hid any trace of his enemy, but he could read that they had not left the trail. And they had not turned the mustangs loose.

The land spread out in smooth rolls of lush spring pasture dotted with tiny yellow flowers as far as a man could see on both sides of the trail. The sky was so big and blue, a man could go swimming in it. Mountains lined the horizons like hazy shadows.

That night they camped in a wash and Cass wanted to be alone. He was hurting and walked to a stand of aspen where he kicked at the dirt and gazed at the endless land.

Texas came to join him in the moonlight. He didn't have to turn around to know it was her. She smelled of lilac water, despite months on the trail. He had always avoided women, but he liked having her near, even though he didn't look directly at her.

"Are you all right, Cass?"

"Yeah."

"Are you angry with Shorty?"

"Why do you ask that?"

"Because he insisted on venison, and he died while you were out looking for it."

Cass shrugged and didn't answer, but she was right.

She stood a little closer, folding her arms in the chill. "My mother died when I was born, so I never knew her. But I was angry when my father died. He drank too much and smoked too much, and he worked too hard. And when his heart gave out, I was furious that he would do that to me, that he would leave me all alone and partners with Thatcher, a terrible man."

"At least you have your uncle."

"Joker's only been here since last year. He came

up to help me, but I can't do anything about Thatcher. Except it doesn't matter now. We're going broke.''

"Why don't you sell out?''

"I guess I've always been stubborn.''

"Yeah, I got the same problem.''

Cass walked from the trees, and she followed. He paused to gaze up at the biggest sky he had ever seen, the stars so close he could throw a loop around any one of them. It was cold and damp, but it was grand country, just as Shorty had promised. His eyes were wet for the first time.

She moved closer. "I heard about all the Darringers.''

"I ain't seen any of my kin since I run off. I guess they didn't turn out much different than me.''

"They say you're all gunfighters.''

He looked down at his hands. "I reckon it's just that we have a natural speed with a handgun. We don't even have to work at it. Must be in the fingers. Man has to do what he does best.''

"So you have a large family?''

"When we was little, me and my brothers was took in when our folks died, down in Texas. But my uncle was land hungry and pushed too hard, and I ain't never learned to take orders. That's why I finally run off. And I ain't never been back. Even with the army, Shorty took the orders, and I just went along with him. Reckon that's a failin'.''

"I'm the same way, unfortunately. But you've never married? You or Shorty?"

"We was always on the move. Shorty didn't like painted women or whiskey, and he kept me clear of 'em."

"No farmer's daughter?"

He stared into the night. "Once there was a mayor's daughter, but she made a fool of me. After that, I figured Shorty was right. Man was better off alone."

"Shorty could have been wrong."

He moistened his lips, uneasy as her hand came to rest on his arm, and he stiffened.

She tugged at his sleeve, turning him toward her, and she stood on her tiptoes, reaching up for his bandanna to tug until his head came down. She pressed her soft lips to his rough cheek, and the sensation rattled his brain so badly, he couldn't move.

"God bless you, Cass Darringer."

She withdrew, her own eyes filled with tears, and as she walked away, he realized no one had ever said that to him, not since he was a boy in church. It hit hard, right down to his gut.

It was more than Texas's kiss that had left him a wreck. When she went back to camp, he wept.

By noon of the next day, they reached the rise from which they could see the town of Lost River, and they reined to a halt. His buckskin tossed its head, and he reached down to stroke the great neck.

Joker and Texas reined up on either side of him.

"Not much of a town," Joker said, "but we got a stage swings our way once a week when there ain't no Injun trouble. circuit judge comes every couple months. They're buildin' up the territorial prison over in Deer Lodge. Sooner or later, the railroad's gonna get up here. And someday, we're gonna be a state."

Overhead, a red-tailed hawk soared so fast it was out of sight before its cry was heard. Longhorn and mixed cattle roamed free on the far ranges in all directions.

The town was west of the river with main street running parallel, north to south. Most of the buildings had wide eaves or roof overhangs to protect the boardwalks.

Aspens and cottonwoods lined the banks of the wide, shallow river. Cass could almost see the trout. Dogwood with new, white, sweet smelling flowers crowded some of the banks.

They rode slowly down the trail and forded the shallow stream where they saw the remains of a washed out bridge. They rode north toward the jail, a frame building set on the left, short of the general store. Other stores and establishments lined both sides of the street, and toward the north end of town, there were saloons, a dancehall and the livery. Wagons and mules lined up along the railings. Cowhands were already arriving for their Saturday night.

Texas and Joker reined up near Cass.

"That's our office over there to the right, just past the bank," she said. "I live in the back of the building. Thatcher has a house out back, and Joker lives with our friend, Mr. Simmons, behind the dancehall, up there on the left."

"Got a hotel?"

Joker grunted. "Over there to the left on the hill, near the church. But you'd get better food at the rooming house up the street, across from the dancehall. That white house. The Barnes family runs it and the general store this side of it, just past the jail."

A man in his shirt sleeves and leather apron came out of the saddlery on their right. "Texas, you'd better be talkin' to Thatcher. Your office was robbed about ten days ago."

She made a face. "They couldn't have taken much."

"No, but they also hit the bank."

Joker was grim. "They catch them?"

"Well, you'd better be askin' the sheriff."

Texas let her hat fall back, her flaming hair shining in the sunlight, her face just as red.

Joker shook his head. "Now we know what them fellas was accused of when they was hanged."

Cass watched them ride on and circle the freight office with the mules following to the corrals behind it, then he turned his stallion to the railing in front of the jail on his left.

"Hey, mister, stable your horse?"

He turned to see a small boy of maybe ten, freckled and blue-eyed, wearing tattered clothes and moccasins. Cass liked youngsters. They were usually wide-eyed and full of wonder, still living their fantasies, so ready to accept the ridiculous in order to have fun.

"Maybe later," Cass said.

"Just ask for me. I'm Bucky."

Inside the solid, well built jail, with its two front windows the only incoming light, he saw two empty cells in the back. The desk was to the right with a bunk near it. The sheriff was playing checkers with another older man at a table near the iron stove, which was set near the left wall. Both wore thick beards and looked as if they hadn't bathed in a month.

"Sheriff, I be needin' your help."

"Later."

"Now."

Leaning back in his chair, the sheriff was getting plenty disgruntled. Yet he could see the grim look on Cass's face and the searing ice in his blue eyes.

"All right, what is it?"

"My partner was murdered a couple days back, southeast of here, and they stole a dozen mustang mares, unbranded, but I'd know them right off."

"You sure it wasn't Indians? Chief Joseph and them Nez Perce went chargin' through here last year, and kept on goin' down through Yellowstone Park and into Wyomin' Territory, but there could be stragglers.''

''Indians don't hang white men.''

''What are you gettin' at?''

''I'd been out huntin'. When I come back, three fellas that had shared our camp was hanged on a cottonwood, and my partner had been beaten to death. They shot me out of the saddle when I was comin' over the hill.''

''So you didn't see these fellas.''

''No, but if I find our mustangs, I'll know who done it.''

''Well, son, it coulda been anybody.''

''Looked like vigilantes. Maybe ten of 'em.''

''Don't know nothin' about it. I just got back in town this mornin'.''

Cass handed him the card. ''Their pockets was cleaned out, but one of 'em gave me this.''

''Railroad, eh? Don't make sense up here. Surveyors come through over twenty years ago, but it's still four hundred miles south to the nearest track.''

The sheriff suddenly leaned forward, fussing as his partner jumped his remaining checkers. Growling, he stood up, walked stiffly to his desk and sat down in his wooden chair, then pointed to another.

''I'm Sheriff Webb. Sit down. Write out your complaint. If you can write.''

Cass laboriously wrote out his story in full, suddenly

grateful for the wirehaired teacher down in Texas who had threatened him into learning, and handed it to him.

"Reckon there are plenty of ranches around here what would buy green mustangs, no questions asked. Maybe you could point me toward a few of 'em."

"You let me handle this, son. What's this? Your name's Cass Darringer? Everybody's heard about you Darringers. I ain't never seen no handbills on you, but weren't you runnin with the Red River gang about the time they was lynched?"

Cass shrugged. "I'd left 'em long before that, and all we did was work for the cattlemen. Now I hear your bank and express office was robbed about ten days ago. You figure that was the reason for the vigilantes?"

The sheriff folded Cass's report. "Well, if it was, they didn't hang the right ones. I got the real culprits over in Target, east of here, two days ago. Had to shoot 'em, but they had the money bags, all right. They'd killed a bank guard, so they was gonna hang anyhow. But I'm right sorry some innocent men got strung up."

Cass pushed his hat back. "Maybe the vigilantes figured out they were innocent after they hanged 'em. Maybe that's why there weren't no papers on the dead. Got any idea who was in on it?"

"Nope, and I'll bet we ain't gonna find out, either."

Cass paused a moment, studying the sheriff's puffy

face and thick beard. The man's eyes were dark and small but plenty grim. There was no telling how much the sheriff really knew. It didn't look like the man was going to be much help.

"Now you listen to me, son," the sheriff growled. "Them vigilantes sure ain't goin' to wanta be caught. You say they shot you out of the saddle. They see your face?"

"One of 'em did. Came up and kicked me good, tryin' to see if I was alive. I played possum. His voice was kind of squeaky, I think, but I was hit pretty bad, so I can't vouch for it."

"Let's hope they don't recognize you. But you go pointin' out who's got the mustangs, they'll know who you are and sure enough want you dead. They'll be plumb worried you saw their faces."

"If I find them mares, I'll find Shorty's killers."

"And a pine box."

Cass spun on his heel and went back outside.

He was reaching for the reins of his horse when he heard a boy's cry. "Let me go!"

Cass looked across the street to where Bucky, the boy he had just met, was being shaken by the hair. A big, ugly hairy man held Bucky and was snarling down at the youngster.

"You was in my way, boy!"

"Let me go, Rufus!"

Cass's face grew hot, his mouth dry. The dirty

stranger was maybe six foot six, big as a grizzly, but nothing could stop Cass as he started across the street. The giant stood watching him approach but kept his grip on the boy's hair. The lad's fingers were clawing at the big hand.

"Let go of him," Cass ordered.

Chapter Two

The big man's mean eyes were as black as his greasy mustache and beard. He was staggering, intoxicated. He laughed at Cass and dropped the boy from his grip. Bucky fell to his knees, then scrambled away. The giant snarled at Cass. As he moved, his big Mexican spurs jingled.

"Maybe you don't know I'm Rufus Poague."

"Maybe you've had too much to drink."

The big man came swaying from the boardwalk to meet Cass in the street, big hands lifted. Smelling of sweat and whiskey, Rufus moved unsteadily toward him. It was obvious the giant could break three men in half at one time. Only his intoxication gave Cass an edge.

Men stood aside to watch. The boy was hiding off to Cass's left, in an alley between the jail and the general store. Two strolling women suddenly darted into the bank across the street.

Rufus moved like a massive grizzly on its hind legs. He roared so loud it hurt Cass's ears. Then he rushed Cass, who sidestepped and plunged his fist into the big belly. With a gasp, the man stumbled past, crashing against a wagon.

Bellowing, the giant rushed Cass once more.

Cass dodged, barely escaping the great hands. It was then that Rufus turned around with wild eyes, fury coloring his face. The big man suddenly reached into the wagon and pulled out a long hayfork. He turned, knees bent, great shoulders haunched.

"Run away from this!"

Moving toward Cass, Rufus looked like a mountain. He kept thrusting the fork in the air toward Cass. His sneer revealed crooked, yellow teeth.

Cass moved carefully, his heart in his throat. Any minute, the iron prongs could pierce his hide.

Suddenly, the big man lunged with the fork. Cass jumped aside and tripped him. Rufus went sprawling across the boardwalk, crashing against the wall with the fork slamming sideways. With a loud roar, the big man turned again. There was blood on his face, his nose mashed.

Raising the fork, Rufus snorted and charged. Cass darted sideways, toward the wagon, then stepped aside. The raging giant crashed hard into the wagon bed. The wagon raised up in the air, then dropped back. Stunned, the big man dropped the fork and grabbed his face. Shaken, bewildered, he yet turned to reach for Cass.

Cass ducked, ramming his fist in the soft belly. The man doubled over, and Cass slammed his fist down on the back of his head. The giant went down to his knees, then fell flat on his face, unconscious. His spurs jingled a moment longer.

Breathing hard and drenched with sweat, Cass looked around. The sheriff was standing in his doorway, watching. The whole town was staring. Including Texas and Joker in front of the freight office and Bucky, still watching from the alley.

"Hey, mister," the saddlemaker called, "he's got a lot of kin. You'd better get outta town."

"No one's ever done that to Rufus," another man said.

Cass drew a deep breath, stood a moment to ease his shocked body, then turned back across the street to his stallion. Exhausted, aching all over, he mounted as he met the sheriff's stern gaze. Then he turned Ranger up the street.

"Hey, mister, can I stable your horse?"

It was Bucky, grinning and anxious. He didn't look too worn from being manhandled. Cass admired his spirit.

"You rub him down?"

"You bet."

"He's a stallion, you know. Might be hard to handle."

"I'll take care of him real good, mister."

The boy took off up the street past the saloons and

toward the livery. Cass rode along behind him, then abruptly pulled aside.

Three wild cowboys rode by at a gallop, stirring dust and waving their hats as they shouted to the wind. They were young, foolish, full of life. Bucky looked after them, envious as he spoke.

"They're from the Lost River Ranch. Langdon's place. Biggest spread around here. I'd sure like to be a cowboy."

"Well, it's a life all right."

"You a cowboy?"

"For a while, yeah. But I've been a scout and trapper and a few other fits and tries."

"Which did you like best of all?"

Cass had to grin. "Bein' a cowboy, I reckon."

"Why was that?"

"You meet a lot of good men."

Cass dismounted at the livery and gave the boy two bits. Then he tossed his saddlebags over his shoulder and took his bedroll and Winchester repeating rifle in hand as he turned to Bucky.

"You know anything about some vigilantes ridin' out of here a few days ago?"

"I don't know nothin', mister—."

"Cass Darringer."

"Wow."

Cass smiled and went back down the street, crossing over to walk past what looked like a town hall with its roof sagging. As he continued down the street, he passed a dancehall and the open lot between it and the white rooming house facing the boardwalk.

Inside, he saw a rocking chair and soft furniture. The place was clean, pretty in fact. White curtains were on the windows. A man could eat on the shiny wood floor. The counter was cleared of any papers. In the back was a staircase. A hearth glowed in a far corner.

A chubby woman about fifty came out of a back room. She was fresh faced, smiling as she went to the desk. She had large brown eyes and fuzzy brown hair rolled in a bun. A full white apron covered her dress.

''Mister, I'm Myrtle Barnes. You must be lookin' for a room. I got one you can have for seven dollars a week. You get a big breakfast and plenty of supper. I don't put up with singin' or hollerin', and you gotta take your boots off at night so you ain't stompin' the floor.''

''You the cook?''

''No, I am.''

Cass turned to see a girl in her early twenties, wearing a blue gingham dress. Her hair was dark brown and in soft curls to her shoulders. Nothing about her face was hard to look at, her eyes large and dark brown.

''My daughter Celia,'' said Myrtle.

Cass nodded and tipped his hat, avoiding the show of his dirty brown hair. He turned to the desk, clumsily filling out the line on the ledger. The woman stared at his name and reluctantly gave him a key as she frowned.

"We want no trouble, Mr. Darringer."

"Won't be none."

"I'll take the money in advance. We read newspapers, just like anybody else, and there's plenty been said about you Darringers. Now, supper's at eight. You ain't on time, you don't eat. My daughter will show you to your room. You want a bath, just holler."

Cass paid her and turned to follow the girl up the stairs. She moved with grace, reaching the landing ahead of him and walking down the hallway.

She stepped aside, pointing to his room.

"I would like a hot bath," he said, unlocking the door. "And some information. You know about the Lost River Ranch?"

"I've only been here a few weeks, but I hear the Langdons run it. I'm told it's very large."

"What about the Poagues?"

"Terrible men. That's all I know."

She turned and walked down the hallway, hurrying down the steps and over to where her mother waited at the desk.

"Mother, isn't he handsome?"

"Celia, he's Cass Darringer, the gunfighter."

"I don't care."

"Well, I do. And your father and I got other plans for you. You think he wants to keep workin' in the store seven days a week? Don't you see how he's failing? The last few days, he's had the shakes. Now you marry one of Langdon's sons and we'll all be better off.''

Later that day, Celia discovered she was out of baking soda. Walking onto the boardwalk in the late afternoon sun, she suddenly stopped with the door still open behind her. Coming toward her were two rough looking cowhands, both in their thirties.

She recognized the taller, swarthy one with a crooked nose as a man named Tully. He had been around before, falling all over himself when he saw her. This time, he was acting even more strangely.

"Well, Miss Celia," Tully said, staggering a bit.

Stiff, annoyed, but wise, she turned to go back inside but stopped in the doorway, watching Cass Darringer coming down the stairs.

"Hey," Tully persisted, breathing on her hair as he leaned close. "Don't run away."

He suddenly reached for her arm, pulling her around. She shoved him away, making a face at his breath.

"Hey," her mother shouted. "Leave her alone."

Tully leaned close to Celia. "I'm gonna kiss you good."

Cass's cold voice was sharp as an arrow. "No, you're not."

Tully kept his hand on Celia's arm, and she pulled back, struggling to be free. She didn't know whether to laugh or yell at this clumsy man, even as Cass came forward.

"Back off," Tully growled.

Cass walked toward him. The man wasn't certain what to do, but he let Celia go. She fell aside and into the sunlight, backing up the boardwalk.

"All right," Tully said. "Come on, mister. I'll tear you apart."

Cass was mindful of the man's heavy build and big hands. Yet he kept walking toward him, because it was a Darringer failing. Even his tyrant uncle had torn into other men to protect women and children.

Rufus had been twice this man's size, and Cass still ached from the fight, but he couldn't stop himself.

Tully sneered, his swarthy face twisted as he wiped his mouth with the back of his hand. Cass was but five feet away.

Tully suddenly lunged at him. Cass sidestepped but caught part of his shoulder, and they went sprawling across the room, crashing to the floor. Before they could pound each other, a heavy broom came down on their heads. Myrtle whacked them good, several times, separating them. They covered their faces with their hands.

"Get outa here!" she yelled.

Both men scrambled to their feet and headed outside. A crowd was already gathering as they faced each other in the dusty street. With his six-shooter, Cass could take him easy. But there was plenty of power in Tully. This was going to be a mess.

Across at the freight office, he saw Texas and Joker coming outside. He was aware of Celia and her mother in the doorway near him as sweat dribbled down his back. Lips dry, he waited as Tully taunted him.

"Come on, mister. I won't hurt you."

They moved around each other like fighting cocks, watching and waiting. Tully's beady eyes were gleaming like hot coals. He was grinning broadly, hands extended as he moved closer.

Suddenly, Tully lunged at him. Cass sidestepped and hit him on the side of the head with his fist. Staggering past and stunned, Tully recovered and turned, wiping his mouth with his big hand.

"That's right, mister. Dance. Maybe you can get away from me. Maybe you can't."

Again, Tully charged. This time they connected, grappling with each other, pounding with their fists, crashing to the ground and rolling over and over. Dust flew around them. The crowd scattered.

Cass spotted the watering trough between the rooming house and the general store. With a wild burst of energy, he broke free of the big hands. He jumped to his feet and backed away. Tully stalked him, grinning broadly.

"I'll break you in two!"

Tully charged. Cass sidestepped, bent his knee, hit

the man on the back of the head and shoved him over his knee and down to the trough. Tully fell in, face down, but his shoulders were too wide and caught his fall. Cass grabbed his head and shoved his face down into the water.

With a roar, Tully came back up dripping wet and climbed out to rush him, both men hitting the ground again. They fought for control, hitting each other as they rolled over their hats.

They were stopped by a barking order from the sheriff, who appeared with a shotgun which he shoved in the big man's gut as Cass rolled clear.

"That's enough, Tully. I've had my fill of your brawlin'. Now get outta here afore I lock you up."

Tully lay on his back, staring at the scattergun.

Celia stood back, hands at her throat. "Are you all right, Mr. Tully?"

Tully was immediately flustered that she asked about him instead of Cass, and it gave him new energy. As the sheriff drew back, the big man rolled over and clumsily got to his feet. He recovered his hat, then glared down at Cass.

"We ain't finished, mister."

"That's Cass Darringer," Myrtle called.

Tully grinned. "No foolin'. Well, my goodness me, I'm scared silly."

Glancing at Celia's smile, shoulders squared, Tully

was satisfied, and he pulled on his hat before walking up the street, staggering a little.

Cass, still sitting in the dirt, felt foolish. He reached for his crushed hat and caught a whiff of lilac perfume. He saw a slender white hand retrieve his Stetson. He wiped his face with his bandanna and looked up at Texas, who was puffing up the crown of his hat, then offering it to him with that dazzling smile.

Wearing a jacket over her frilly chemise and riding skirts, her hair shining like a Texas sunset, she giggled despite herself. He liked it.

Joker came over to stand near her. "You all right, Cass? That was your second fight, and you look plumb wore out."

"And dirty," Texas said.

Cass took his hat from her slim fingers, his face hot. He glanced at the sheriff who was walking away with the crowd. Myrtle and her daughter were still in the doorway, watching.

Texas nodded toward the freight office. "Come along, Mr. Darringer. Join us for some coffee."

Cass struggled to his feet, hurting all over, and walked as steady as he could between her and Joker. Horses crowded the rails ahead where the saloons lined the main street. Every cowhand in town would be having their Saturday night hoot. Some would make trouble.

The sun was already sinking low in the west as they

crossed over to the freight office. Inside, they faced a long hardwood counter cluttered with paper and books. Behind it were two desks and some tables. On their left was an iron stove with a coffee pot steaming.

"Unless you'd rather go up the street for a drink," Joker said.

"I'd rather have coffee."

"That Tully," Joker said, "he's crazy in love with Celia Barnes, but he can't talk to her. Now, I seen Rick Langdon hanging around that girl, so I figure Tully ain't got a chance."

"Don't sell women short," Texas said.

They sat at a table in the back of the room where Texas served coffee. Cass felt dirty and was hurting all over, knowing he was going to be plenty sore come morning. He glanced at Texas, who was smiling, and then at her uncle.

"Why the name Joker?"

"Used to be a riverboat gambler. When my brother died, I come out here to keep an eye on Texas, and see that Thatcher kept his hands to hisself. Now we come back from Salt Lake and find out six hundred dollars was taken out of here. Thatcher claims they broke in from the back, same time they robbed the bank, but I think he just took the opportunity to pocket it himself."

Texas nodded. "But we'll never prove it."

Joker stretched in his chair, and he looked at Cass

as he spoke. "Your head seems all healed up, but you keep gettin' in fights, you'll end up the way we found you."

"Did anyone recognize you?" Texas asked.

Cass shook his head. "I ain't sure. The man what kicked me is probably the only one who could. But all I know about him is he's got a kind of squeaky voice."

"There's a few in town like that," Joker said. "You need more than what you heard when you had a concussion. But everyone knows you're here by now, and why, and the guilty are going to want to get rid of you before you sniff 'em out."

"My uncle's right," Texas said.

Joker got up and stretched. "My bones are weary. See you tomorrow, Cass. Watch yourself."

When Joker was gone, Cass felt a little uncomfortable being alone with Texas, but he was worried about her and this Thatcher he kept hearing about.

"How'd your father get mixed up with Thatcher?"

"My father had some money, and Thatcher had a freight business he wanted to expand, so they became partners, and we moved up here about three years ago. We started hauling from Salt Lake up through Virginia City and to these parts, and business was good while my father was alive. He had papers drawn up so he'd be sure I got his share when he died."

"But you're not doing so good now."

"I think Thatcher is stealing, but I can't prove it."

"You plannin' to tell me your real name?"

"It's Texas. Texas Rafferty. My father named me."

"You know much about the Lost River Ranch?"

"Just what Joker told you, that the Langdons own it. There are two sons. The father is tough as nails. The mother is never seen."

"And the Poagues?"

"Well, they hang around town a lot. Five of them. Rufus and his cousins. Don't think they have much of a spread. Back in the cliffs somewhere back of a canyon called Whiskey Gulch. Everyone's afraid to go there. I think Rufus' wife even went back east to get away from him."

Cass downed his coffee. "Thanks."

As he turned to walk out the front door, she followed him, and they moved onto the boardwalk, in the twilight. She smiled at him and touched his arm.

"I'm sorry I laughed at you. I've never had any brothers to make fun of, and you looked so silly, sitting there on the ground."

"I reckon I did."

"Here comes Mr. Thatcher."

A swarthy man with a slick black mustache, wearing a frock coat and fancy vest, was coming toward them. He walked with a swagger and had narrow eyes, shaded by a small brimmed hat, and Cass took an instant dislike.

"He don't look like no working man."

"Shh. He does the books mostly and gets the orders."

Cass stood quiet but irritated as she introduced them. Thatcher was grim, his nose twitching, mouth curving down at the corners. He smelled of some kind of perfume.

"So you're Cass Darringer. Seems to me I heard you was runnin' with a bunch of outlaws. Most of 'em got hanged, ain't that right?"

Cass didn't answer, his face grim.

Thatcher tipped his hat to Texas and went inside the freight office, slamming the door behind him.

"Real friendly," Cass said.

"He doesn't like men to talk to me."

"Maybe I'd better stick around until he leaves."

"Shh. Here he comes."

Thatcher came out with an order book in hand, glared at them both and went down the street toward the bank and saddlery. Cass wanted to run after him and smash his face, but Texas touched his arm.

"Don't worry about me, Cass. It's you we have to watch out for. You've set yourself up as a target."

"I'm not a patient man."

He tipped his hat and walked up the street toward the noise and laughter. Every one of the three saloons had at least thirty men inside, playing cards and telling stories. The dancehall across the street was not much more than a saloon, but it had a piano and the only women. He could see them being dragged around by hopping young cowboys.

Inside one of the saloons there might be someone bragging about how he made some extra money with a few wild mustangs. Cass walked back to the first saloon, and was about to enter when he saw a figure coming along the boardwalk. It was Sheriff Webb, carrying a shotgun.

They paused, facing each other as night fell.

"What're you up to, Darringer?"

"Just lookin' around."

"There's always some young fella lookin' to make a name for himself. You go in there and let it be known who you are, sure as heck there'll be shootin', and then I gotta haul out some carcass and have it buried, and I ain't lookin' for that kinda work, so why don't you bed down?"

"I ain't sleepy."

The lawman slowly lowered his shotgun. He lifted his free hand and scratched his thick beard, studying Cass carefully. A short but stocky man, the sheriff seemed afraid of no one. Yet he was not a likeable man.

"All right, Darringer, go on inside, but don't say I didn't warn you. And if I were you, I sure would keep my mouth shut."

"Any Langdons in there?"

The sheriff grimaced and peered over the swinging doors. "Reckon not. Some of their hands, maybe."

As the sheriff turned and walked away, Cass shoved the doors open and walked inside. The noisy men were too busy to pay Cass any mind. He wandered over to the bar, then leaned on it, gazing around the smoke-filled room.

Cass shook his head at the barkeep and stood, unnoticed by the busy hands, until a gruff voice spat through the air.

"Hey, Cass Darringer."

Those who heard became suddenly quiet. Many faces turned toward Cass, who paused, his back to the bar. Rising from a corner table was Tully, who was waving at him.

"Come on, Darringer. I'll buy you a drink."

Cass stood still a long moment. It didn't make a lick of sense, but he slowly moved across the room, making his way to the table where four older cowhands and Tully sat with cards being shuffled. A sixth chair was dragged up, and Cass stood near it.

"Sure, sit down," Tully insisted, a grin on his swarthy face, cup of coffee in hand. "I'm soberin' up, but you can have anything you want."

"I'm not a drinkin' man, but I'll have some of that coffee."

Cass moved the chair so his back was to the wall, causing everyone to shuffle their own chairs. He was sitting across from Tully now as the annoyed barkeep brought him some coffee, which looked days old. Tully was cheerful.

"Fellas, I want you to meet my good friend, Cass Darringer."

The four other men were mustached and red from the sun. They didn't seem one bit impressed with Cass's reputation. Good cowhands had enough of their own world to worry over. Fast guns were just a short-lived nuisance, and Cass had to grin. He declined to join in the poker game but sat enjoying his coffee, even though he was certain it would rot his insides.

"So," Tully said, "you'll soon be eating Celia's chow. She sure is a pretty little thing."

Cass frowned. "That so?"

"Hey, don't get on your high horse. Fact is, I been tryin' to talk to her but never could manage it. This time, I'd had a few drinks and got brave, that's all. I ain't never learned how to act around ladies, and that's a fact."

"Yeah," said one of the hands, "ole Tully talks to women like they was horses."

Tully grinned at Cass. "Hey, I sure pounded you, didn't I? Too bad the sheriff had to come along. You'd have been mince meat."

"Don't be too sure," Cass said.

"What're you doin' in town anyhow?"

"Lookin' for some stolen mustangs."

Tully and his friends gazed at each other with a shrug.

"Darringer!" came a shout.

They all looked to the center of the saloon where men were scattering in every direction. Left by himself was a young man with a strapped down holster. He was standing with feet apart, his hat pushed back from his smooth brow. He had a small chin and large nose. His eyes were pale and narrowed. He wore a fancy red vest.

"I'm callin' you out," the youth said.

The men at Cass's table began to move, clearing the area. All except Tully, who merely stood up and aside. Cass slowly, carefully, got to his feet.

"I got no reason to fight you," Cass said.

"You're a dead man, Darringer."

"You got a name?"

"Yeah, the Arizona Kid."

"It'll look right fancy on your tombstone."

"You don't scare me none."

"You got any kin?"

Slowly, Cass moved around the table but kept his back to the wall. He had faced upstarts like this before. Sometimes he could bluff them out of it. It was becoming clear, however, that the Arizona Kid was not one bit afraid. That made him mighty dangerous.

They were maybe fifteen feet apart. The room had fallen silent around them, everyone crowding to the walls, behind the tables or the bar. Smoke lingered in the air, stinging their eyes.

"You work for the Langdons?" Cass asked.

"Yeah, that's right."

Someone coughed in the back of the room. It unnerved Arizona. Skin crinkled around his eyes. His mouth tightened suddenly.

Arizona's hand went for his six-gun, quick and sure, bringing it up swiftly. Before he could level and fire, he stopped, six-gun pointed at the floor, and he caught his breath. He was staring at Cass's Army Colt. He hadn't even seen Cass's hand move.

"Go ahead," Cass said.

Slowly, his face reddened, Arizona lowered his six-gun back into the holster. Hatred burned in his eyes. Grim, furious, he carefully backed toward the door. Humilitated, he moved outside as Cass holstered his Colt.

For a long moment, the saloon was silent, watchful. Then chairs were shuffled back into place, and it became noisy once more.

Cass had turned toward the table when Arizona suddenly and wildly charged back inside, firing his gun, a bullet whistled by Cass's ear.

Chapter Three

Everyone dove for cover, chairs crashing over backward.

Spinning and jumping aside, his Colt leaping into his hand, Cass fired, dead sure.

Arizona gasped, wide-eyed, doubling up with blood high on his chest, gasping for air. He dropped to his knees, staring at Cass with disbelief on his young face. Void of color, the gunman fell face down, dead as he hit the floor. His white fingers still gripped his six-gun.

"Man, you got him dead center," a cowboy said.

Cass drew a deep breath, his face burning. He looked at Tully's admiration. Glancing around the room, he saw a mixture of fear and distrust. Another gunman was dead, and nobody seemed to care, except Cass.

"Didn't even see your hand move," Tully said.

Shaking his head, Cass holstered his weapon and walked toward the swinging doors, knowing they were all watching. Tully followed him onto the boardwalk. It was cold out and dark beyond the lamp hung at the entrance. Cass was still hot and damp all over. He hated the pain he had to suffer now.

"How come you're so fast?" Tully persisted.

"Runs in the family. Like a curse."

"Wish I had that problem."

"No, you don't."

"Watch out," Tully whispered.

They could see the sheriff coming in the moonlight, the big man puffing to a halt in front of them, shotgun in hand. Cass looked from Tully to Webb, who was snarling as two men carried Arizona out and down the street. The lawman was pointing his shotgun at Cass's middle.

"All right, Darringer, I warned you."

"It was a fair fight," Tully said. "Arizona called him out. Cass had him cold before Arizona could clear leather. And so Arizona left, but all of a sudden, he came chargin' back inside like a crazy man. Cass didn't have no choice."

The sheriff mulled it over. "Well, all right, but you get outta here, Darringer. Them boys will all be spoilin' for a fight now."

"Not likely," Tully said. "Arizona didn't have no friends. Rex Langdon, he hired 'im, but even Rex didn't like 'im much."

Tully and Cass walked past the sheriff, who turned into the saloon to ask a few questions. They could hear the words "fair fight" being repeated.

"You'd better turn in just the same," Tully said. "The sheriff, he means business."

"You know anything about those mustangs?"

"Nope, but I saw some in the corral at the ranch last night when I come back from workin' cattle."

"There a pinto mare with 'em?"

"Yeah, matter of fact there was."

"You got any idea how they got there?"

"Cass, I don't know nothin'."

"What's Langdon like?"

"A grizzly, tough as they come, but he's got a sick wife, and he spends a lot of time with her. His sons are always spoilin' for trouble. They're the ones hire gunmen like Arizona. And Silvers."

"Silvers?"

"You know him?"

"I know of him."

"They say he's killed a lot of men in gunfights. You're fast, but you don't like killin', and Silvers does. If I was you, I'd forget them mustangs."

"My partner was killed. And three innocent men were hanged."

"Yeah, everybody's talkin' about it, but nobody knows anything. But whoever done it, they'll be pickin' you off so you won't figure who they was. Them boys don't care much how the slate gets clean."

They paused in the moonlight in front of the dance-hall, glancing inside. Some of the hands were paying a dime a dance to hold "high class" women, all dressed modestly with their hair done up in curls. The piano was playing a waltz.

"I know them women from the saloons over at Target, east of here," Tully said. "They all wanta get married now. Why do you figure that is, Cass?"

"Well, they'd sure go for a prize like you."

Tully rubbed his chin. "You think so?"

A shabby, old man who looked like a prospector was haunched in a chair near the window. The bartender, skinny and bald, was standing at his table talking to him.

"The fellow sittin' down, that's old Simmons," said Tully. "Hasn't struck it rich yet. Ain't got no kinfolk, but he comes to town to see Texas. He's crazy about her. And he's great friends with Bucky, that orphan kid. The bartender is Swaps. I think he's grubstaked ole Simmons a few times."

"I didn't know Bucky was an orphan."

"Yeah, his folks died of cholera on their way to Oregon a couple years ago. But he just don't fit in nowhere, even with the Barnes family, where he's stayin'. Reckon he never got over losin' his folks."

Tully went inside, but Cass declined, his heart heavy as he headed back along the street. He had come here to find Shorty's killer. He was in no mood to fight every challenge.

Inside the rooming house, he had to force himself to enter the dining room where five clean-swept plates were being lifted by a weary Celia. He removed his

hat. They were alone in the big room, and she paused, smiling at him.

"I'll set you a plate. Just don't tell my mother."

The stew and biscuits were delicious. He ate heartily, despite himself. When he finished, he looked up to see her standing there. She was smiling as she spoke.

"I learned to cook real fancy at school. But I have to make do with what's in the store out here."

"It was mighty fine."

He stood up, taking his hat in hand. She was a good looking woman, but she was the marrying kind. Cass carefully backed toward the door. She was crowding him.

I want to thank you for helping me with that cowboy, that Tully. You were wonderful."

"He gave a good account of hisself."

She smiled, her arms about her. "Yes, he did. But he's always so dirty."

In his room, Cass lay back on the pretty blue spread that covered the narrow bed. The room was small, but it was cheerful. He had a window overlooking the street. He drew his six-gun and held it across his chest as he fell asleep.

In the morning, Cass enjoyed a good breakfast of bacon and eggs with more of the wonderful biscuits. The other boarders were three men. One was elderly, named Torry, another, Rugby, about forty, was built like a bull and spent a lot of time watching Celia.

The third man was Jenks, pink faced and about thirty, dressed like a dandy with a little bow tie, and introduced as the sheriff's nephew, visiting from the east. He was also wearing a fancy gold watch chain dangling from his vest, and he bragged constantly about his travels, irritating Cass.

"I seen that first Kentucky Derby, back in '75. Even bet on the winner, Aristides. Less than three minutes around, and I got me a bundle. And I saw President Grant, big as life. Why, I done kissed the Liberty Bell. And I played polo in New York City, over at Dickel's Riding Academy."

Myrtle was entranced by his stories, leaning toward Jenks with eyes wide. Cass couldn't see this man as the nephew of the crass, rude, insolent and dispassionate sheriff, and yet, next to Jenks, Webb was a nice fellow.

Cass left the room and headed into the sunlight, pulling on his hat and settling his Colt in its holster. He was wearing a clean blue shirt and needed a shave.

He could hear the church bell ringing up in the hills west of town and near the hotel. Wagons were headed up toward it. Women were in their finery as children danced around them. Men wore dark coats. The Barnes family had invited him, but he had declined, figuring he couldn't face a fire and brimstone preacher until his job was done.

At the barber's, he had a shave and had his dark

brown hair trimmed collar length. He felt better and moved back into the sunlight, pausing to glance at the lazy river. Then he turned to watch a tall, husky man come out of the sheriff's office across the street. The lawman was right behind him.

The barber, a funny little man with endless chatter, came to stand beside Cass. "That's Ross Langdon. He's the big he-bull in these parts. Don't be tanglin' with him."

Cass studied the rancher. The man had a strong set of shoulders and thick chest. He wore a dark coat and sported fancy boots. His hat was small brimmed over a square, grim face with a red handlebar mustache.

The barber chuckled. "I guess the sheriff just told him how you took care of his hired gun. Probably never thought anybody could take Arizona, 'ceptin' maybe Silvers."

Abruptly, Langdon turned and looked straight at them. The barber ducked back inside. Cass stood stiff in the sunlight, watching the rancher come across the street toward him with long strides. Langdon looked mean as sin and plenty mad. His voice was thick and raspy.

"You Cass Darringer?"

"That's right."

"I hear you shot down one of my men. Arizona."

"It was a fair fight."

"Maybe it was, maybe it wasn't."

"I had no way to stop it. But you got some mustangs that was stolen from me. Whoever took 'em, killed my partner and hanged three innocent men."

"Sheriff just told me. We bought a dozen mares, all right. But they wasn't branded."

"Who'd you buy 'em from?"

"I don't know. There's a bill o' sale at the ranch. Rex, my oldest, bought 'em from some fellers passin' through."

"One's a pinto mare. Got white fetlocks and a cross on her shoulder. Maybe I'll just ride on out and take a look."

"Not without me," the sheriff said, moving toward them.

"You're takin' your job mighty serious," Langdon growled at the lawman.

And so it was that the three men were soon riding north out of town, following the shallow lazy river, then turning northwest to pick up the wagon road. Scattered trees hosted yellow-bellied sapsuckers, blue-birds and woodpeckers.

It was a beautiful country, wide and green, the hills ever rolling toward the distant mountains where bear and mountain lions roamed. Pines dotted the ridges, and one could envision mule deer and elk in the lush meadows. Cattle grazed in every direction, and a bull was bellowing in the far off hollows. Cold wind blew lightly in their faces.

"Gonna rain afore long," Langdon said, and he turned to Cass. "I sure am takin' a fancy to that stallion. Wanta sell him?"

"No, thanks," Cass said.

"Langdon, I've been meanin' to talk to you about somethin' else," the sheriff said. "Your boys have been gettin' out of hand. They think they own the whole territory."

"That's on accounta what I have in mind."

"And what are you goin' to do about the other ranchers?"

"I settled where I had plenty of water, but I need every bit of that free grass. I got the law of customary range all on my side, and I ain't gonna budge."

"You didn't answer my question."

"Listen, sheriff, why don't you concentrate on who's been rustlin' my cattle? You talk to them Poagues yet?"

"Sure, but they just laugh it off. And I ain't never seen nothin' on their place but scrub cattle. Tracked a herd in there once, but they must have some way out through a back trail. I didn't feel much like hangin' around to find out."

"Well, if I ever catch 'em myself, I won't be needin' your help."

"We've already had too much vigilante ridin' around here. You let me handle it."

Langdon grunted and rode on ahead.

The ranch was spread over high ground near the lazy river. It was well cared for, the buildings all painted. The house was a Texas house with two parts, a covered opening in between. Cattle and horses grazed on the surrounding hills. In the corral, two grizzled hands were riding among the twelve mustangs mares, their long ropes ready.

At the fence, Langdon called to them.

"Hold up there, men. You seen my boy Rex?"

"He went huntin' mule deer with his brother," one of the men replied. "Left afore daylight."

"Bring that pinto up here," the sheriff said.

Langdon nodded to the men. Both tossed their loops over the mare's neck, scattering the other mustangs as they brought it over to the fence. Nervous, it had good bloodlines, distinguishing it from the others, a black crosslike mark was on its shoulder, and white fetlocks.

"She's one o' mine," Cass said.

"You coulda seen her somewhere's else," the rancher growled.

"Or you could be receivin' stolen property," the sheriff said to Langdon. "You'd better be showin' us that bill o' sale."

They rode up to the ranchhouse, dismounted and left their horses at the railing. Inside, they found a fire still burning in the hearth. The living room was well furnished with leather chairs and a sofa. Fine paintings of the West were on the walls.

Langdon went to a large safe in the corner and unlocked it by spinning the combination. Then he took out a small metal box, which he opened, drawing out a folded paper. He handed the document to the sheriff, who studied it.

"Well, it's a bill o' sale, all right. But it's signed with an X."

"I can't help it if the man couldn't read."

The sheriff glared at the rancher. "Well, I'm figurin' we'd better talk to your boy Rex."

"I'll send him into town tomorrow mornin'."

"See that you do."

The sheriff turned and walked outside. Cass paused, gazing around the room, envious. Then he looked at the rancher's scowl.

"I ain't tryin' to cheat you, Mr. Langdon. I only want what's mine. And I want justice. If your son didn't kill my partner and hang those railroaders, maybe he knows who did."

"You saw the size of my spread. You figure we care about a bunch of scroungy mustangs?"

The rancher's eyes narrowed under thick brows. He looked mighty grim, and he bit hard on a chunk of tobbaco.

"That's going to rot your teeth," Cass said.

Langdon looked at the tarry chunk in his hand, then unexpectedly grinned. "That's what my wife says."

Cass didn't want to like Langdon, but he did and

hoped the man was not involved in the murders. He turned and walked outside where he mounted and rode with the sheriff, back toward town. It was mid-afternoon and getting plenty cold with a rising wind. Dark clouds appeared on the western horizon.

"Langdon's pretty hot about this," the lawman said.

"What about his sons?"

"Well, aside from the old man never givin' 'em any real money, they work pretty hard and mind themselves all right. Oh, a brawl now and then. And a lot of gamblin'. Rex, the oldest, he's got the most brains. Rick, he goes along on anything Rex wants."

"You figure the Poagues are rustlin' their cattle?"

"I wouldn't put it past 'em, but I got no proof. Langdon's overstocking his ranch and spreadin' out over every inch o' free grass he can claim. Up here, it's whoever's makin' the best use, if he gets there first."

They reined up as a dozen Langdon men approached, some bent over in the saddle. Tully was in the lead, grinning at them.

"Hey, Cass, you still in one piece?"

Cass nodded, waving as they passed. The last rider pulled his horse over in front of Cass's. The man was tall, lean of face and body, his eyes surrounded by loose skin. His Colt rested low and handy on his hip. He wore a black leather vest, and his smile was sinister.

"So you're Cass Darringer."

"Back off, Silvers," the sheriff warned.

Cass sat quiet in the saddle, his stallion restless and pawing the ground. This man was no Arizona, full of splash and daring. Silvers was a gunman who knew how to kill without hesitation. He was dangerous, his voice like ice.

"You ran with the Red River boys. I knew some of 'em afore they were hanged. They told me you was faster than any of 'em. So I'm wonderin' now, whether they was right. I hope you won't be leavin' town afore I have a chance to find out."

"Silvers," the sheriff snapped, "get out of here."

Still smiling, the gunman tipped his hat and rode past them, joining the others and heading north.

Cass realized he had held his breath. He collected himself, riding on with the sheriff.

"He has a reputation," the lawman said. "You can figure he'll be lookin' for you, sooner or later."

"All I want is justice. And my horses."

"No show down?"

"I didn't come lookin' for Silvers."

"You got some idea you can change, is that it?"

Cass nodded, riding on ahead. He didn't feel he had to explain himself. He didn't trust anyone, including the sheriff, who was the least likeable man he had ever met.

Back in town, Cass was at the rooming house in time for supper, but Jenks's bragging sure spoiled it. The elderly man, Torry, seemed to ignore him, and Rugby never listened, his mind always on Celia. Cass later found himself wandering in the moonlight, first to the dancehall where he peered inside to see Joker and Simmons telling yarns at a table near the swinging doors.

"Biggest grizzly I ever saw," Simmons was saying. "Why, this room wouldn't be big enough for his teeth."

Cass ventured across to the saloons, but he saw only a few men there, not one looking mean enough to be a vigilante. He turned and walked back to the freight office.

There were lamps burning inside, curtains holding in most of the light. He heard a woman's cry from inside.

"Let me go!"

He heard a struggle, a chair falling, a slap and a body hitting the floor with a crash.

"You ain't got smart yet," a man snarled.

Cass tried the latch. The door was locked. He drew back and kicked hard. The door flew open, and he walked in, grim and silent, surveying the scene in the office.

Texas was on one knee against the far wall near the stove. She was wearing a blue, high collared chemise under a blue jacket with a dark skirt, lustrous hair spilled about her ashen face. Her blue eyes were wild, and she appeared breathless.

Standing nearby was Thatcher, out of breath, in a

fancy white shirt with ruffles. Cass hated ruffles, and he hated this sleazy dude. Thatcher turned angrily.

"What do you want here, Darringer?"

Cass held his hand out for Texas, who rose slowly and moved toward him rather quickly, stumbling once. She took his left arm and moved behind him.

"Cass, it's all right. Mr. Thatcher's been drinking."

"Did he hit you?"

"Yes, but I'm not hurt."

Thatcher was grimacing. "Get out of here."

"You owe this lady an apology."

"Lady? Hah. You're wet behind the ears, fella."

Just then, Joker came in from the outside, but Texas waved him back and went to stand at his side, his arm encircling her.

Thatcher moved behind his desk and sat down, right hand out of sight. The desk had no panels. Four round legs supported a frame merely six inches deep. Cass figured a gun was being aimed at his middle.

"I hate your guts, Darringer."

"Yeah, well, I hear you been keepin' the books around here. Maybe that's why this outfit's goin' broke."

"Why you dirty sidewinder. You callin' me a thief?"

"Sounds like it."

The skin around Thatcher's eyes was crinkling, a

sure sign. The muscles in his right arm twitched under his coat.

As the bullet came under the desk with a blast, Cass darted aside, six-gun leaping into his hand and firing.

Cass's shot hit Thatcher high in the chest. Round-eyed, the man gripped the desk with his free hand, and his mouth fell open as he dropped back and slumped dead in his chair. Gunsmoke hung in the air, followed by a long silence.

Cass stood still a moment, certain the sheriff would be along plenty fast, then turned to look at Texas. She was standing with light from the office lamp glowing soft on her face, her eyes round and glistening, Joker's arm around her, keeping her from rushing over to him.

"Glad you was here," Joker said.

Sure enough, the sheriff came charging from across the street, carrying that blamed shotgun, and pushed his way past Texas and Joker.

"All right, Darringer, I got you this time."

"Look behind his desk, sheriff. On the floor."

The lawman walked into the office, moved around and knelt, then stood slowly with the dead man's gun.

"It was fair and square," Joker informed him.

"All right, Darringer, so you're clear on this one, but I'm gettin' mighty tired of pickin' up after you."

"Then get my mares back. And find those killers."

"Just as fast as I can."

"And have someone haul off that carcass."

"I'll move 'im," Joker said, and he went over to grab Thatcher by the coat collar at the nape of his neck, dragging the body unceremoniously out the front door and onto the boardwalk.

Then Joker returned to sink down on a chair, exhausted. The lawman looked at Texas, shaking his head. She was standing with her arms about herself, obviously shaken.

"Why don't you sell out and go on back to Texas where you belong?" the sheriff asked, reaching to touch her reddened cheek. "Unless you're gonna marry one of them Langdons, you're fair game around here. I can't be lookin' after you."

Her eyes were brimming with tears at his concern.

Cass was startled by the man's unexpected gentleness.

The sheriff glared at him, then walked to the door and moved outside where a few men had gathered around the body. Soon Thatcher was being hauled away.

Cass studied Texas a long moment. He was going to worry about her, but he had other trouble on his mind.

"What's this about the Langdons?"

"Rex has been hanging around a lot."

Cass turned and walked around the counter. She followed him outside into the moonlight. He paused, one hand on the door, wondering why she no longer made him so nervous.

"Thank you, Cass."

Abruptly, she took his arm, stood on her tiptoes, and reached with her free hand at his neck to pull his head down. She kissed him on his rough cheek, her lips like sweet velvet, and he nearly fell apart. Then she drew back with a gentle smile and folded her arms in the chill.

"You don't like women much, do you, Cass?"

"They scare me plenty."

"I want us to be friends."

He nodded, then swallowed hard and turned away, his knees full of jelly. He walked along the boardwalk, listening to the loud clunk of his boot heels.

Moving into the soft dirt of the street, he continued toward the livery. Lanterns on each side of the entrance were turned low. Men were snoring in the loft.

Cass walked to the stall where his buckskin stallion was standing, and he found Bucky stroking its nose. The boy turned to grin at him.

"Ain't you got a home?" Cass asked.

"Yeah, with Mrs. Barnes, over at the store. I work there and got place to sleep in the storeroom."

"Don't she worry about you?"

"I'm eleven already. I'm gonna get me a real job. I can be a wrangler, soon's I'm big enough."

"Who said?"

"Tully, he said."

"Well, come on. You're goin' home."

In the morning, Cass arose early, and after breakfast, he went to Barnes' store to buy new clothes. Bucky was cleaning pots, and Cass made it clear to Barnes, the elderly, grumpy, bespectacled clerk, that he was only buying there because of Bucky. Barnes was much older than his wife Myrtle.

In fact, the storekeeper's hands were trembling constantly, and strangely enough, he had a squeaky voice. Yet Cass couldn't see this mild little man with a lynch mob.

Bucky was talkative. "Mr. Darringer is after some mustangs got stolen. Vigilantes killed his partner and hanged three men out there."

Barnes seemed very agitated and kept dropping his pencil. Myrtle came over to take it from him.

"Now, honey, you've been working too hard. And you need your rest," she said.

When Cass left, Bucky at his heels, he walked into drizzling rain, carrying his bundles and about to turn toward the rooming house.

"Darringer!"

He knew the call, the sound, the challenge. Slowly, he turned.

Chapter Four

Standing on the boardwalk in the drizzling rain, wearing a new leather coat, a bundle of new clothes under his left arm, Cass paused and turned to look into the street.

It was Rufus Poague, dirty, unkempt, his huge bear-like body in a haunch as rain dribbled off his hat. The man's greasy black mustache hung down on his beard. He had to be six foot six. He was staggering, but this time he was not intoxicated. His big spurs still jingled.

"You're lookin' at Rufus Poague," the man called, beating his chest. "Ain't no man ever bested me at nothin' when I was sober."

Cass stood waiting, his right hand dangling near his Colt. He had escaped this man's fury once before, but this time, he knew he would not be so lucky.

"I hear you're some kinda gunfighter. You want to have a shootin' match with that toy? Or you wanna fight like a man?"

"I got no reason to fight you, Poague."

"You got me when I was drunk. Now it's my turn."

Cass looked past him to the men sitting on the porch

across the street. Four huge, ugly bearded men, probably his kin, were watching, a jug on the knee of one
of them. They looked plenty dangerous. Mountain
men, out of place here. It wasn't likely they cared
whether a fight was fair. If Cass was to best Rufus,
the others might jump on him.

Looking the big man over, Cass decided a hand to
hand fight with this grizzly was foolish. He could feel
his back snapping already.

"I'm not fightin' you, Rufus."

The giant staggered closer, pausing some fifteen feet
away. The drizzling rain was dribbling from his narrow
brimmed hat. His big soft belly was Cass's only hope.

"Listen here, Darringer, I'm gonna mash you
good."

"I don't have time for you."

With that, Cass waved Bucky back inside, then
turned and started up the street toward the rooming
house. He was aware of spectators gathering under
nearby roof overhangs. Rain was coming down hard
now, pounding the boardwalk. Rufus' voice bellowed
like a bull.

"Darringer, I'm gonna tear you apart."

Cass kept walking. It was then he saw Texas coming
out of the bank just ahead on the other side of the
street, a long umbrella in her hands, hat thrown back.
She stood under the eaves, staring. Suddenly, she
called to him.

"Cass, look out!"

He heard the thumping, running footsteps behind him on the boardwalk, which was shuddering under the weight. He spun about, dropping his bundle. The giant was rushing him at full charge. Cass jumped aside and tripped him.

Rufus roared as he crashed to his knees and sprawled on his hands in the heavy rain. Clumsily, he got up and turned around, eyes gleaming with anger as he snarled. He looked big as a barn. Cass was determined not to show fear, but he had a knot in his stomach. Rufus's voice was deep, throaty.

"All right, Darringer, if you wanta dance, go ahead. But once I get my hands on you, you're a gonner."

"You know, Rufus, I'm beginning to think this is personal."

"You gonna talk or fight?"

"Could be you killed my partner and hanged those fellows and tried to kill me. And stole our mustangs."

"You're loco."

But Rufus was wiping his mouth as if thinking a little too hard. Then the big man moved closer, huge hands outstretched, yearning to grab Cass by the neck. Cass moved cautiously in a circle. Both men were wet from the cold, darkening rain. The street was turning to mud.

"Cass, be careful," Texas said.

Rufus Poague was losing patience. He began to close

in on Cass' movements. Dancing aside, Cass knew he
either had to run or face those big hands. He darted in
quick, slamming his fist deep in the man's belly.

Rufus gasped, doubling up as Cass jumped aside,
but the big man's hands suddenly clamped down on
Cass' left arm, jerking him off his feet.

Before Cass could react, Rufus had lifted him in the
air and thrown him bodily to the street. Cass fell on
his back in the mud, breath knocked out of him, and
he lay in a sweat as he watched the big man flex his
muscles.

Suddenly, Texas rushed out of nowhere and slammed
her umbrella on the back of Rufus's head. He didn't even
bother to turn around, figuring it was about as big as a
mosquito bite, but he swung his arm backward, catching
her in the middle and knocking her back against a post.

That made Cass furious, and he started to rise, but
the giant charged him, and he rolled aside, frantic,
even as Rufus crashed down on his knees with a grunt.

''You scared of me, Darringer?''

Sliding around in the mud and water, Rufus tried to
get up, his back to Cass, who got to his feet and put
his boot hard on the man's rump, sending him sliding
further into the mud.

With a roar, Rufus scrambled to get to his feet,
slippin and sliding. Again, Cass kicked him in the rear.
Snarling like an animal, the giant crawled further away

and rolled on his side, reaching out for the next kick. Cass backed away.

"I'm gonna break you in half, Darringer!"

Cass held his breath as Rufus got to his feet. They were both soaked with mud and rain. He started to run at Cass and slipped, falling toward the ground. Cass slammed his fist in the man's face, cracking the big nose. Dropping to his hands, shaking his head, the giant was stunned.

"All right," said the sheriff, appearing with shotgun in hand. "That's enough."

Cass stumbled back a few steps. "Sure took you long enough."

"Well, I don't want you to hurt ole Rufus."

Holding his bloody face, Rufus was frantic. "He broke my nose!"

Cass glanced at Texas, who was leaning against the post with a bent umbrella. She looked out of breath but unhurt.

Cass pulled his hat down tighter, rain pouring from the brim and down his buckskin coat. He felt chilled, weary, and he hurt all over. Moving to the boardwalk, he picked up his bundles, already soaked.

The sheriff lowered his shotgun. Furious, Rufus Poague stumbled around, then crossed over to where his kin were waiting. Some of them were laughing.

"Darringer," Webb said, "I've got better things to do than keep you out o' trouble."

Cass shrugged and walked under the eaves where Texas was standing. She was pale, staring at him, her eyes round.

"Oh, Cass, are you hurt?"

"Came close. What about you?"

"He knocked the wind out of me. But I'm all right." She tried to open the umbrella, but it was crooked. She stared at it and laughed.

Cass had to grin. "What did you think you were gonna do with that spindley thing?"

"Protect you, I guess."

They gazed at each other as rain ran off the roof a few inches from them. It was strange how his fear of women was forgotten when he was around her. He wanted to move closer, but his boots wouldn't budge. Just gazing at her stopped him cold. She was gorgeous, and he sure did like her freckles.

She blushed under his stare, pulled her hat on and lifted her skirt, then walked in the mud, her boots sinking deep, toward the freight office.

He dragged himself along at her side. When she reached the door and moved under the eaves, he stepped out of the rain to stand near her. Their hat brims were dripping between them, and she was smiling at him almost shyly.

He was uncomfortable. "You were in the bank. Anything wrong?"

"Thatcher was stealing from the outfit," she said.

"Mr. Krutz said our deposits were changed to bank drafts, a little at a time, until there's almost nothing left. He doesn't know what Thatcher did with the money. And he refuses to give me a loan to pay the men. So I guess I'll be closing down in a few months."

"You want me to talk to him?"

"Cass, people always fight you. If my being a woman didn't work, nothing will."

"Can Joker help?"

"He came here to help me with not much more than the shirt on his back."

It was then that they saw two men riding into town, haunched over in their slickers. One was Ross Langdon, big and mean, spitting tobacco in the rain, his red handlebar mustache twitching.

Texas pressed back against the wall of the office, and she nodded to them as they tipped their hats. She turned to Cass, watching his face.

"That's Ross Langdon. And his son Rex."

Langdon's son was a large man in his mid twenties. They headed for the sheriff's office down the other side of the street, and Cass made a move to follow.

Texas touched his arm. "Why don't you wait?"

But Cass took off in the rain, boots sloshing in the mud. When he reached the jail, the two men were already inside, their mounts shuddering at the hitching rail. Entering, closing the door behind him and grateful for the warmth of the iron stove, Cass saw the Langdons already seated at the lawman's desk.

"Come over here, Darringer," Ross said. "My boy's gonna set you straight."

The sheriff leaned back in his chair. "Rex, Mr. Darringer here claims them mustangs you bought was stolen."

"Maybe they was," Rex said, removing his wet hat. He had a big face like his father, but he was clean-shaven. His dark eyes were sinister while his manner was pleasant, like a tame wolf. "But I bought 'em fair and square."

"And who from?" the sheriff asked.

"Two drifters come by. One was skinny. The other what signed was short and mean lookin'. Maybe what he told me to write wasn't his real name."

"They say where they was from?" the lawman asked.

"No, but they was headed for Oregon. Soon's I give 'em the money out o' Pa's safe, they took off."

Cass stood nearby, listening, wondering.

"Well, now we got us a problem," the sheriff said. "Mr. Darringer claims those mares was his. Rex, you claim you bought 'em from someone else."

"We want to do what's right," Ross Langdon said. "If those men killed Shorty Greene and took the mustangs, then we got no claim. But all we got is Darringer's word."

Cass was grim. "I'll still sell 'em to you."

"We already paid two hundred dollars," Rex said.

"All we got here," said the sheriff, "is a justice of the peace. But maybe he oughta listen to this."

Ross shook his head. "All he knows how to do is marry folks or put a drunk in jail."

"So what do we do?" Rex snapped. "We're out two hundred dollars. You wanta give Darringer the mares when we don't even know if they're his?"

Ross turned in his chair, looking up at Cass. "Would you take a hundred for the lot?"

"They're already broke to lead. They're worth ten apiece."

Reaching into his pocket, the rancher pulled out a sack of gold coins, setting out one hundred twenty dollars. The sheriff wrote a proper bill of sale, copying the descriptions from the first draft. The document was signed and witnessed.

The Langdons left without further discussion. Cass sat down, staring at the closed door, shaking his head.

"That was too easy, sheriff."

"Don't give me no trouble, son."

"You know that Rex and his brother could have been with the vigilantes and taken the mustangs. If the old man is so stingy with 'em, what better way to get some cash? All they had to do was buy the mares from themselves. Maybe their Pa figured it out for himself and that's why he set things right."

"You got your money, now head out."

"I'm not leaving 'till I know who killed Shorty."
Cass pulled his hat down tight, standing slowly.

"Listen to me, Darringer. You'd better stay out o' trouble."

"I've been jumped by Tully and twice by Rufus Poague. I've had to kill two men. And I only got here Saturday. All I want is Shorty's killers. Now what do you know about Barnes? He's got as squeaky a voice as any man here."

"That old man? Forget what you're thinkin'."

"A lynch mob could've given him some guts. Maybe he was tryin' hard to show his wife he was a man."

"She's a lot younger, but she's a good woman. Ain't likely he'd have to prove himself to her."

"Maybe not, but I ain't leavin' no stone unturned."

"By now, whoever come up on the hill and kicked you, he's probably recognized you, and they ain't gonna rest until you're dead. You're a walking target."

"You know any better way to smoke 'em out?"

The sheriff just shook his head. Cass walked outside, pausing in the shelter of the overhang to gaze at the heavy rain. The fireplace at the rooming house would be welcome just now.

Instead of returning to the house, he walked over to the freight office and peered inside to see the lanterns turned up bright. Texas was at the counter, shuffling papers. When he tapped on the window, she let him inside, then returned to stand behind the counter, all the while smiling at him.

He leaned on it with his elbow. "You gettin' along?"

"I'm all right."

"Maybe you oughta have a woman stayin' here."

"I'd have to think about it, but I have my uncle around most of the time to look after me."

"Looks like you been goin' over your books."

"So far, it looks like Thatcher was lying about everything."

There was a tapping at the window, and it was Simmons, peering inside, hat in hand. They let him in, and he fussed about Cass being alone with Texas.

"Don't worry," she said, touching his beard with affection. "Cass looks after me quite well."

"Yeah, I heard about you. One of them Darringers. And you shot Arizona and ole Thatcher."

"He shot Thatcher because he was putting his hands on me," she said.

"Blast," the old man said, pounding his fist on the counter. "I wish I'd have been here."

Simmons gazed at her with adoring eyes, his thick brows drawn together. He wasn't very tall, and he was stooped, age catching up with him rather quickly.

"I'm goin' back to the hills. You gonna be all right?"

She squeezed the old man's hand. "Yes, and I'll miss you."

Simmons grinned, showing bad teeth, and then he sobered as he looked Cass up and down. "This fellow gives you any trouble, you let me know."

After Simmons left, Texas leaned on the counter with a gentle smile. "I don't know why he likes me so much, but I do like him. I guess we all like people who really care about us. And I guess that's why I like you, Cass."

She was leaning toward him, and he could smell lilacs. Her skin was soft and peach colored, her gaze so warm, it caused him to start sweating.

He turned and started toward the door, but she had moved around the counter, and her hand caught his arm. He paused, swallowing hard. Slowly, he turned, looking down at her. She barely was as tall as his shoulder. Her slim fingers still rested on his arm, white against the leather of his coat.

"I want to help you, Cass. With the Langdons."

"No, you stay out of it."

"But Rex tells me things, and I—"

"No. I don't want you hurt."

Slowly, she withdrew her hand. Her eyes were wide and glistening in the lamplight. "I'll be careful, Cass. I promise."

Frowning, he hesitated, fighting the urge to reach

for her. Then he turned and headed for the door, anxious to be outside.

And while he was dodging her and the rain, the Langdons were riding back toward their ranch. The cold wind was blowing the wet in their faces. Ross Langdon had been silent, casting angry glances at Rex.

Now as the ranch buildings came into view, the rancher could wait no longer and turned to glare at his son.

"Where did you get them mustangs?"

"Pa, I told you. Two drifters. You was out with the men. Just me and Rick were on the place when they come."

"You paid too much. Or maybe you didn't pay nothin'. You playin' faro again?"

"Pa, we ain't never lied to you. And faro, well, Rick and me just have a little fun, that's all."

"You got a real need, Rex. Sometimes I wonder what's got into you. When you was a youngster, you was my partner. Now you're always workin' against me."

"You treat us like kids, Pa. We're grown men. I'm near to twenty-six. I want a wife and family. You gotta start sharin', Pa."

"You get a wife, I'll think about it."

"What'll I offer her? Wages? Come on, Pa, you got to put our names on the spread. You gotta do it now."

"You boys are gonna get it all when I die, but you

ain't earned nothin' yet. You don't like it, you can ride on out.''

''You can't get by without us, Pa.''

''I don't need nobody. You oughta know that by now. And if I ever find out you were part of a lynch mob and faked a bill o' sale, just to get a couple hundred dollars out of me, I'll ride you out of here myself.''

''We ain't done nothin' wrong, Pa.''

''You never rode with them vigilantes?''

''Not us, Pa.''

There was a long moment when Rex drew a deep breath and became silent, looking for a way to appease his father. Finally, he spoke with a forced smile.

''We been keepin' them Poagues and the others off our range. We ran off some squatters. We know there's been rustlin', and we've worked hard, tryin' to catch 'em, and we'll get 'em sooner or later. I figure we been earnin' our keep. And now I got me a lady friend, Pa. Texas.''

The rancher grunted. ''Texas Rafferty? She's probably the most beautiful woman in the territory. She wouldn't give you the time of day. Now when I was younger—''

''I been talkin' to her some. She likes me, and you'd like her.''

''Well, that be the case, you bring her around.''

Ross Langdon grunted and rode on ahead. Rex reined up, sighting his brother Rick down by the corrals. He turned his horse and rode over to where Rick was perched on the top rail. The rain had stopped, but the wind was cold.

Rick was a little younger, fresh faced, more boyish. He had the same dark eyes, but he was more light-hearted.

"Hey, Rex. How'd it go?"

Looking around to be sure they were out of earshot, Rex leaned forward in the saddle. "Pa bought them mustangs from Darringer. A hundred and twenty dollars."

"He got cheated."

"Keep your voice down."

"You think Pa suspects what we done?"

"You never know what that old man is thinkin'."

"But we was just at the hangin', that's all. All we did was watch what the Poagues and the others was doin'. And it was Rufus killed that old man. All you did was get the one comin' over the hill."

"Yeah, well, the one comin' over the hill was Cass Darringer."

"They killed a Darringer?"

"No," Rex snapped. "He was still alive when we rode off. Blast that Barnes. He said he was dead."

"Holy cow. We're in trouble."

"Nobody's gonna say we was there, on account of they don't wanta hang either. Except I'm gettin' worried about Barnes keepin' his mouth shut."

"But the mustangs—"

"It was the Poagues brung them along, not us. But I'm figurin' we can't push the old man any further. Meanwhile, I'll be goin' back to town tonight. Gotta see Texas. I marry her, Pa will loosen up with the money."

While the brothers talked in lŏw voices out by the corral, Ross Langdon went into the house. His silver-haired wife, puffy and tired and semi-invalid, was lying in bed. She looked up as he entered.

"Come sit with me, Ross."

He sat near her and took her hand. "You all right, honey?"

"I'm worried about our boys. Rex, he's in some kind of trouble, and Rick, he does anything Rex wants."

Before he could answer, Rick's voice carried into the house. "Pa, we got company."

The rancher went back through the living room and to the open doorway where Rick was standing just outside. Ross closed the door behind him and glared at Rufus Poague, whose nose was bandaged. The big man was seated on a big black gelding, and he looked grim. At the hitching rail, Rex was lounging as he chewed on a twig.

"We got to talk, Langdon," Rufus said.

"So, talk."

"That Cass Darringer is gonna cause a lot of trouble.

We gotta get rid of him. And I figure your hired gun Silvers can do it.''

Ross Langdon folded his arms and leaned on the door frame. ''I ain't worried about Darringer.''

''You got a short memory. That last hangin', we shot Darringer's partner dead. And we thought we got Darringer, not knowin' who he was, but now he's sniffin' us out.''

''That's your problem. I wasn't at the hangin'.''

''Your sons were.''

Langdon kept his gaze fixed on the giant in the saddle. He wouldn't look at his sons as shock settled into his gut, his whole body chilled as if he was rolling in snow. His face was void of color, and he was stiff and angry, his voice raspy.

''Listen to me, Rufus, I don't know if you're lyin' or not, but what you're tellin' me is, you got them mustangs and brung 'em here, and it was you sold 'em to my boys.''

''Don't matter now, Langdon. If you don't want your boys to hang along with the rest of us, you'd better set Silvers on Darringer and get rid of 'im.''

Rex nodded. ''Maybe Silvers can take him.''

Rufus straightened in the saddle. ''Well, I've had my say.''

There was a long silence, and Ross's gaze was piercing, sending flashes of danger as his fury rose.

After a long moment, Rufus turned his black horse

and rode away toward the east. He sat straight and grim in the saddle. When he was out of earshot, Rex turned to his father.

"What we gonna do, Pa?"

"Why didn't you tell me you and Rick were in on the lynchin'?" the rancher bellowed. "I have to hear that from some grizzly?"

Rex was pale, his eyes glassy. "Pa, there was a bunch of us. Me and Rick, we just sorta got caught up in it. And Rufus claimed they was guilty. The sheriff was out of town. It sort of got out of hand, that's all. All we did was follow along and watch."

Rick nodded. "We didn't know they was innocent 'til after they was hung and we took their papers off 'em and saw they really was from the railroad. They'd been flashin' new money, all right, but they didn't have much on 'em. Not enough for the bank robbery."

"So you had to bring the mustangs here and draw up a phoney bill of sale to get money out of me? If you weren't my own sons, I'd turn you in and see you hang."

Rex stiffened. "Pa, if you'd share what you got, somethin' like that wouldn't happen. You got to make us partners."

"Over my dead body."

Furious, the rancher went back in the house. His sons were shaken and looked at each other, then walked together toward the corrals. Alone, they paused.

"Rex, Pa is really mad."

"He'll get over it. Maybe he'll get to thinkin' how stingy he's been with us."

"Maybe, but right now, I'm worried about Darringer. If he figures out we was in on the killin's, we're dead."

"We'll get Darringer first."

"And Pa's gonna kick us out, ain't he?"

"Not when I get through figurin' what to do."

While the brothers talked, Cass Darringer was pacing in his room, knowing he was hot on the trail but unable to be certain where it was leading. Later that night, he tugged his hat down tight and left the rooming house. The night was cold and damp, and the street was still muddy as he crossed over to the other side.

Lanterns hung under the eaves at a few of the stores and all of the saloons, but not at the freight office.

He paused at the window, but it was dark inside.

Suddenly, a bullet thudded into his back near the left shoulder. With a gasp, he dropped to his knees, spun around and rolled on the boardwalk, sixgun in hand.

Chapter Five

Cass rolled against the wall of the freight office, out of the moonlight, his left shoulder racked with pain. Colt tight in his right hand, he lay still, watching.

Suddenly, there was a flash of light from the alley across the street, between the rooming house and the general store. A bullet crashed into the wall near his head. Cass fired, twice, his shot slamming into something wooden. He fired again and saw movement in the alley as someone was running away.

Jumping up, ignoring the pain and bleeding, Cass charged across the street, dodging back and forth. Once he reached the alley, he flattened himself on the wall and peered down through the dark passage toward a group of buildings.

Darting forward, he stumbled over old machinery and came out the back. The night was protecting the backshooter. After a fruitless search, he returned to the alley.

Cass fell against the wall of the store, holstering his gun and reaching over to clutch his left shoulder. He was in pain and losing blood fast. He drew a deep breath and went as far as the edge of the buildings, peering forth. No one came outside.

Except the sheriff, coming up the boardwalk, shotgun in hand. Cass staggered out of the alley and caught hold of a post under the eaves of the store. Dazed, he could only frown at the hurrying sheriff who came to an angry halt.

"Blast you, Darringer."

"Backshooter."

Cass bent over, still clutching the post.

Men were gathering now. Joker, half dressed, came to his side and took his right arm, holding him steady.

Lamplight was suddenly aglow in the freight office window, and now Texas was hurrying outside in a blue wrapper, shivering and staring, a Winchester repeater grasped in her hands.

"Get him to the doc," the lawman finally grunted.

Joker helped Cass across the muddy street to where Texas was waiting, her rifle lowered as she came to meet them but Joker didn't want her out in the cold, not in her nightclothes.

"Cass will be all right, honey. You go back inside. I'll get him up to the doc's."

She hesitated, until she saw the crowd appearing now on the boardwalks. She took a moment to gaze into Cass's grim face, knowing he was hurting as she smiled sadly.

"How are we ever going to keep you out of trouble, Cass?"

He managed a grin, shaking his head as Joker marched him down the boardwalk to the doctor's office, which was over the offices where the justice of the peace did business.

At length, Cass was in his room, stretched out on his bed on his right side, left arm in a sling. Joker was worried, sitting on his chair, and fussing.

"You're taking a lot of chances, Cass. You're a target. And this is no place for you to hide while you're healin' up."

"Got any ideas?"

"Bunk with me at Simmons' shack. He's out of town, so there's an empty bunk. We go now, no one will know you're there."

And so it was that they slipped out of the rooming house in the middle of the night, leaving by the back steps and heading across the lot to the back of the dancehall where Simmons had his shack. The prospector had left town, and Cass gratefully stretched out on his bunk and fell asleep as Joker covered him.

In the morning, he awakened to the scent of lilacs.

Sunlight from the window cast a glow on Texas's flame red hair. She was wearing a blue cape over a gingham dress and was kneeling at his side. She leaned over to adjust his pillow, and she smelled wonderful.

"Do you hurt?" she asked.

"Like sin. What are you doing here?"

"Joker had to go out to the store. He's bringing you food."

He watched her as she drew up a chair and sat near him. Maybe he kind of liked her worrying about him.

"Cass, you were talking in your sleep, but I couldn't understand the words."

"I was dreamin' about Shorty."

She laid her cool fingers on his hot brow, then wet a towel in the nearby basin and pressed it over his forehead. He thought he would die at her touch. She was warm, sensitive, reaching out to him, striking all the right chords.

"Are you gonna marry Rex Langdon?" he asked, startled by his own words and frowning as he gazed up at her.

"Rex? He hasn't asked me, but he was here last night. I only saw him for a minute. He said he had business."

"Figures."

"You think he was the one who shot you? Maybe I can find out when I see him again."

"You stay away from him. He could be dangerous."

She smiled at him as she moved the towel and pressed her hand to his forehead. "You're cooler now."

Joker entered with a box of groceries. "You're about

to have some very expensive eggs. And some ham. But we got to have some fresh coffee.''

"I'll make it," Texas said, rising and going over to the stove.

Joker fried the eggs and ham, and the three of them ate breakfast together. Cass was propped up with pillows and blankets on his right side, and he ate hungrily, but when he turned to Texas, his brow was deep with lines.

"I worry about you alone in that freight office."

"Don't worry," she said. "I keep the doors locked at night, and I have a revolver. And Joker checks on me."

"You bet I do," Joker said.

Texas nodded, cup in hand. "It's a shame what Thatcher did to the outfit. And my father worked so hard and put all his money into it."

"It's gonna be all right," Joker said. "We're getting a lot more orders now that Thatcher's gone. Seems nobody was trustin' him no more. We'll be gettin' more wagons and mules. Now if Simmons would just start a gold rush in the hills around here, we'd be rich in a hurry."

Texas smiled. "He might be disappointed if he finds gold. I think it's the searching that makes him happy."

When they were gone from the shack, Cass finished his coffee and lay back, weary and in pain. As he closed his eyes and began to dream, he thought of Shorty and their nights around the campfire.

While he slept, Rex Langdon was out at the ranch, cornering Silvers near the tackroom.

"Silvers, I want to talk with you."

Silvers walked behind the building with Rex. Silvers was quiet, waiting as he rolled a smoke. At length, Rex spoke, his voice low.

"Silvers, I want you to take care of Darringer."

"That so?"

"Are you interested or not?"

"I figured on doing that in my own time. My gun's worth a lot more if I take him down."

"Well, I'm the one who got you hired."

"Rex, you don't have enough money. Unless you rustle a few more head of your father's cattle. What's Poague paying nowadays?"

Fury turned Rex's face beet red. He had thought his nighttime cattle operation was a secret. It was a long while before he could speak, and then his voice was wavering with anger.

"Listen to me, Silvers. This place will be mine someday. I'm the oldest. I got plenty comin' to me."

"Why do you want Darringer?"

"Never you mind."

"Well, if you want me to take Darringer afore I'm ready, you'll have to come up with something solid."

Rex swallowed hard. "How much?"

"A thousand."

"Well, you know Pa would never let me get my hands on that, but listen, how would you like to be part owner of this place?"

"Seems to me, your father has it all."

"He's an old man. He's goin' to die someday anyhow, and I'm tired of waitin'. He'd be easy for you to gun down."

There was a long silence. Silvers let the words hang in the air as he lit his smoke. Rex was dark with anxiety, his belly churning, trying to bite back his words.

Finally, Silvers spoke. "You'll have to deal with that yourself. But you get me a thousand, I'll take Darringer."

"I'll get it, somehow. But you repeat anything I said here tonight, and you'll be sorry."

Silvers smiled, drew on his smoke, puffed a little and turned away, leaving Rex to stew in his fury and frustration. After all was said and done, maybe Rex would have to find a way to get rid of Silvers as well.

The next morning, Cass Darringer awakened from a deep slumber. Sunlight fought to creep through the curtains of the front window. Joker slept across from him, fidgeting in his sleep.

Hurting, a little dazed, Cass sat up carefully. He ran his hand over his lined brow, finding his fever gone. He pulled on his hat and gunbelt, but it took great effort to pull on his boots with his left shoulder hurting.

Rising, he left the shack quietly, but in the open lot between the dancehall and the rooming house, he came face to face with Texas. She was wearing a heavy coat over her dress, cascades of lustrous hair about her face and shoulders. He had to catch his breath at the sight of her.

He was stuck in his boots, unable to move. She came toward him, pausing but a few feet away.

"You're not well enough," she scolded.

"I'm goin' to the roomin' house for breakfast. Unless you want to join me at Joe's Cafe up the street."

"I'd love to have breakfast with you."

As they moved in the morning light to the boardwalk, Cass looked up and down the empty street. Whoever had backshot him had escaped but could try again.

They crossed over to the busy Joe's Cafe with its white tablecloths and frilly curtains. Inside, two skinny women were serving a dozen hungry men, while an old man was cooking in the back. The tables were long and lined with benches.

Texas and Cass sat at the end of one, facing each other. No one else was in earshot. They ordered a hearty breakfast of bacon and eggs, which cost a dollar apiece, having come a long distance packed in lard.

"I'm in the wrong business," she said. "I should raise chickens and hogs."

"Yeah, me, too."

"I've changed the sign on the freight office. Rafferty's Freight & Express. If we get out of debt, Joker will be a partner.''

As they lingered over their coffee, he saw lights dancing in her eyes. He liked what he saw and was annoyed when Sheriff Webb suddenly appeared and sat at his side.

The lawman tipped his hat to Texas and ordered coffee.

''This mornin', one of our merchants was found dead in an alley. He was stabbed in the back. Celia Barnes's father.''

Texas was distressed. ''He was a nice old man. Why would someone kill him?''

''Well, they didn't go through his pockets, so it weren't robbery.''

Unhappy, she stood up, excused herself and left them.

The men, having stood with her, now sat down, and they watched Texas go into the street. Webb was shaking his head.

''What the devil does she see in you, anyhow?''

''Must be my pretty face.''

''Maybe she just likes ugly men.''

Their humor fell flat. Neither man could figure why Barnes was killed, but Cass knew there was a connection.

''Murdered right after I come to town. Another co-incidence? Sheriff, I know it's tied in with Shorty and the lynchin'. And Barnes could have been the man with the squeaky voice.''

The lawman stuck his pipe in his mouth. ''Wild guesses. That's all we got. We're writin' a dime novel here.''

Cass stood up slowly and walked to the door. The sheriff followed, and they moved to the undertaker's just up the street past the saloons, where they paused.

Coming across the street was Myrtle Barnes, dressed in black with a veil. At her side, clutching her mother's arm, was Celia, wearing a black cape. They were both badly shaken. Trailing was Bucky, his face colorless.

Celia paused at Cass's side. Her eyes were red from crying, and she slid her hand into his as her mother went inside the undertaker's, followed by the sheriff. Bucky stood nearby, restless, kicking at a stone on the boardwalk.

Celia looked up at Cass. ''I'm glad you're here.''

Suddenly, Myrtle Barnes shrieked inside the building.

''Get out of here, sheriff. My husband didn't know anything about any killings.''

Like a lamb, the lawman came outside and frowned.

''It's a dead end, Darringer.''

Celia went inside to join her mother, Bucky trailing. Drained, weary and with his shoulder hurting, Cass turned to look up and down the now busy street. It was a warm day.

Cass was uneasy, hurting, and he needed to go to the freight office. He had two friends there, Joker and Texas, and sometimes a man just needed to talk. But Joker was giving him a lecture before he could hardly fill his cup with coffee.

"You've already had fistfights. You've had to kill two men, and someone's shot you in the back. Now they got Barnes, who had to be one of 'em. If you don't give up this hunt, you're going to be as dead as a doornail."

Texas reached for her hat. "Joker and I have planned a picnic for today, just to get out of town for a while. And we're taking you with us."

Cass was startled, but she wouldn't back away. Before he knew it, they were riding out of town.

Texas was astride a sorrel mare, and when she rode on ahead at a lope, she was riding like a Comanche, so much a part of the animal, she responded to its slightest muscle.

By early afternoon, Texas had chosen a spot on a hill, high above the surrounding land with a view of the river. Cottonwoods and aspen shaded them as bluebirds sang in the branches. Joker pointed to the northeast where white sandstone cliffs were streaked with red.

"That's the way to Whiskey Gulch, and the Poague's stronghold."

Blankets were spread. Joker was already half asleep.

Seated there in the shade, nursing his sore shoulder and watching her fuss over the luncheon, Cass felt comfortable, his appetite high, but Texas apologized.

"I'm afraid I picked all this up at Joe's Cafe, except for the cookies. Have you ever been on a picnic?"

"Just campin' on the trail. But not like this."

He lay back, resting on his right elbow as he ate, his wound still aching as he gazed across the land. Soon Joker was asleep and snoring, and Texas moved closer to Cass.

"Have you ever been to San Francisco?" she asked.

"No."

"Do you suppose the streets are really paved with gold?"

"I don't know. But I've heard they have as many as a hundred ships inside the bay. Tall ships. I think it would be something to see."

"I'd like to go there someday. I'd like to see the ocean. I've never seen anything bigger than Salt Lake."

He drank the cool water she had brought and lay back on his right side, half asleep. He gazed at the sky through the new leaves of the cottonwood. Dark clouds had appeared, and a buzzard was sailing past. He closed his eyes in contentment.

As he dozed, he was aware of something cool on his lips, and he opened his eyes. It was Texas, kissing him gently, bending over him with her long soft hair brushing his face, her lips like velvet on his, sending wild sensations through him. He felt he was dying from pure joy.

His right hand went up, settling deep in her hair and feeling electricity through his fingers, drawing her down so she rested against him. He kept tasting her sweet lips and lost all reality, in a daze from which he could not return.

Now she was slowly backing away. He stared up at her shy smile as she sat back on the blanket, away from him, leaving his lips feverish. Flushed, she was embarrassed at her boldness, and he was devastated, drained.

She busied herself gathering up the cloth and dishes, folding everything into the bsket. It was getting cold as the wind came up and drifting clouds appeared.

Joker awakened to bring the horses around, and when they were packed up and wearing leather coats, they led the animals down to the river to drink. His stallion was nosing the sorrel mare's neck, and Cass pulled it away. Texas knelt to trail her fingers in the crystal clear water.

It was starting to drizzle. The sky was darkening.

Joker and Cass were standing together, watching her. As Cass abruptly knelt to put his own hand in the water, a shot rang out, the bullet whistling where he had been and striking Joker on the side of the head.

Texas screamed. Joker gasped, dropping.

Cass spun about on one knee, six-gun in hand.

Chapter Six

Texas was fighting hysteria and crawling in the grass along the river, trying to reach Joker who lay prone with a bullet in his head. Cass was on the ground, flat on his stomach, looking up the hill and down the river as light rain began to fall.

"Stay here," he muttered, pulling Joker's revolver and sliding it over to her.

Moving quickly to his stallion, he holstered his sixgun, pulled his Winchester from the scabbard and mounted. He turned downriver at a gallop, certain the bullet had come from the aspens on the rise of a far knoll.

When he reached the rise, he rode into the trees, figuring whoever had shot Joker was already gone, and he was right. He leaned from the saddle and checked the grass for signs. A horse had been there and been ridden back over the hills, down to the wagon road.

It was pouring rain now, and fury was setting in, churning his insides. He reined the stallion about and headed over the hills, back down to the river.

Texas had spread a blanket over Joker. She was

standing still as a statue, rain dribbling off her hat band, Joker's Colt in her hands. When Cass dismounted, he saw the tears in her eyes, the way her lips were quivering.

They rolled Joker's body in a blanket and put him over his saddle. They tied him down, and her hands were trembling and white with chill in the rain.

She looked up at Cass with agony, then moved to slide into his arms, her face at his chest. He felt her soft body sobbing against him as he rested one hand on her shoulder in the softness of her hair.

Riding back toward town in silence, leading Joker's horse, Cass glanced at her bent figure. She would be lost without her uncle, and Cass felt responsible.

The rain was heavier now. Lightning flashed in the clouds heavy on the horizon. It seemed forever before they were in town, riding down the quiet street and pulling up in front of the sheriff's office.

Once inside, she hurried to the little iron stove to warm her cold hands.

The sheriff was seated near it, playing checkers with Jenks, Cass's fellow boarder and the sheriff's nephew. The pink faced dude with his silly smile was jumping the lawman's checkers.

Annoyed, Webb looked up to glare at Cass.

"Now what?"

"We were shot at down by the river," Cass said. "I figure the bullet was meant for me. They got Joker instead. It was one rider, but I lost his trail on the wagon road.''

''Dadburn it, Darringer. Ever since you got here, there's been nothin' but trouble. Now Texas is on her own. Who's going to look after her?''

''Anyone come ridin' hot into town in the last hour?''

''Not that I know of.''

Texas was still shivering from cold and shock, keeping her hands over the stove. She was angry now, her face pink.

''Sheriff, you've got to find that man.''

''I'll take Joker to the undertaker,'' Cass said. ''And I'll take care of the horses.''

Texas nodded without looking at him. Grim and weary, Cass went back outside into the rain. When he had done his sad chore with Joker, he took the horses to the livery.

Late that afternoon, he attended the brief funeral for Joker, who was buried near his brother on the hillside. The drizzling rain fell on Cass, Texas and the small crowd. She was wearing a black cape over her dark blue dress.

They walked down the wooden path to the boardwalk, where they paused to look at the muddy street as darkness fell. It was now pouring hard. A gentleman would offer to carry her.

She gathered her skirts. ''It's all right, Cass. I know your shoulder is still hurting.''

But he turned and lifted her in his arms just the same, resting her against his right shoulder and barely using his left. Her hair brushed his face as she nestled in his embrace, her hand tugging at his leather coat, and he felt her sob.

He struggled through the mud until they reached the other boardwalk in front of the freight office and under the eaves, out of the rain. When he set her down, she turned to gaze up at him with tears on her face.

"Cass, thank you for being here."

"If I hadn't come chargin' into Lost River, Joker wouldn't be dead."

"Joker was on your side, Cass."

When she had gone inside, he stood alone on the boardwalk in the dark. Despite the cold, he was damp with sweat. He turned and walked back toward the rooming house and paused by the water trough.

Suddenly, shots rang out from across the lot, one tearing into his right thigh, another catching his left arm as he swung about. The third shot missed as he dived down behind the trough, six-gun in hand, sinking in the mud.

Across the street, Texas came running out of her office with a rifle, but he waved her back. Instead, she knelt in the darkness behind a post, watching, and she was in the line of fire. He waved at her again, but she refused to move.

He crawled to the end of the trough to gaze up the

empty lot. Another shot crashed into the wood near his head. Cass saw the flash of light from behind the rooming house. His wounds still in shock, he sprang to his feet and ran toward it, dodging sideways in the rain.

Another bullet spun by his ear. Cass charged to the side of the rooming house, dropping to one knee against the wall. He had no cover, but the man had stopped firing.

Boots sliding in the mud, he raced to the back of the building in time to see a dark figure hurriedly climbing the stairs to the second floor. The man turned and fired, missing. Cass fired back, hitting dead center.

Like a great bird, the man twisted and fell forward into space, over the railing. He hurtled downward, crashing to earth like a rock, sprawling in the mud in front of Cass.

There was only moonlight until the back doorway of the rooming house opened a crack at first, then all the way, lamplight spreading on him and the wounded man. Standing there was Torry, the elderly boarder. Myrtle was right behind him, her mouth open, and Rugby was behind her.

Cass knelt and rolled the man over. It was Jenks, still clutching his six-gun, his face white and strained. He glared up at Cass with narrowed eyes and twisted mouth as he muttered.

''Missed again.''

"You shot at me before?"

Jenks nodded, closing his eyes. Blood came from his mouth. He was still alive but mortally wounded.

"Why, Jenks?" Cass asked, shaking him.

Jenks closed his eyes, choking on his own blood, and went unconscious, head rolling to the side. Texas came running up, dress rimmed with mud, rifle in hand and her face and hair wet from the rain.

Myrtle was upset. "This town hasn't been the same since you got here, Mr. Darringer. And now look what you've done. You've shot the sheriff's nephew."

Texas took Cass's arm and led him inside, where Celia helped her get him to a chair in front of the blazing hearth.

Torry and Rugby dragged Jenks into the back hallway. Then Rugby went for help while the two women led Cass over by the hearth. Texas pulled off his leather coat and his dripping hat, and he sat down as she fussed over his left arm until she saw the blood on his right thigh.

"Oh, Cass," she said anxiously.

"Just what did you think you were doing over there with that rifle?"

She sniffed back her tears. "I was trying to save your hide."

Despite his pain, he smiled at her. "Yeah, you sure were. And it was right thoughtful."

When the doctor and sheriff came, they went into

the back hallway with Jenks. The sheriff stayed with his nephew, but the mustached, aging doctor came back inside the room.

"Nothin' I can do for Jenks. He's conscious, but he's going fast."

The medic worked on Cass's thigh, cutting the heavy cloth of his britches. "Just a flesh wound. Bullet went right through. Elevate it until mornin'. Your arm's barely creased. And I see your shoulder's healin' fine."

The doctor put Cass's left arm back in a sling. The sheriff walked through with his eyes averted and didn't say a word as he went outside. Before leaving, the doctor confirmed Jenks was now dead and he would send the undertaker. Later, Torry came to join Cass and the women at the fireside.

"The sheriff just left town," the old man said.

"Convenient," Cass grunted.

"Why, Cass," said Celia, "that's not a nice thing to say. The sheriff knows Jenks tried to kill you. He must have other business."

"Rustlin'," the old man said. "When I was outside, some rancher came ridin' in full speed. His boys were already hot on the trail. Some place east of here, near Target."

Cass was in no mood to listen, and he struggled to his feet. Texas helped him over to the stairs and up to the landing, but he stopped her at his door. He gazed down at her lovely face, wondering when this would all be over so he could really take a good look.

"Are you going to be all right?" he asked.

She smiled. "You're asking me? Every time I turn around, someone's shooting at you."

He was hurting too much to say anymore and went into his room, locking the door behind him and turning up the lamp. He lay back on his bed, glaring at the ceiling in the pale light. Jenks was the sheriff's nephew, had probably been one of the vigilantes, and was likely the reason none of them had been arrested. Now the sheriff had left town.

Weary, he slept at last. In the morning, his leg was plenty sore. He hobbled down the stairs for breakfast, and when he later pulled on his hat and coat, heading for the front door, Myrtle followed him.

"When you're all healed up, Mr. Darringer, it might be better if you left town. As long as you're here, people are going to be murdered all around you."

He didn't feel like arguing, because he'd about had it with Lost River. After two bare knuckle fights, he'd killed three men, Arizona, Thatcher and Jenks, and he still didn't have the answers.

Grim, he stepped outside into the cold where the sky was clear, the street soaked and muddy. He needed a ride. He had to get out of this town before the doctor stopped him.

At the stable, the keeper helped him saddle Ranger

and he managed to mount despite his wounds. He rode north, following the wagon road, then turned west into the hills, riding through great herds of Langdon cattle, waving back at the distant cowhands. Now he rode through a canyon where his stallion picked its way through rocks and brush.

Unexpectedly, he came out onto a wide meadow where a little creek sang its way south. It was pretty as a picture, surrounded by high hills. Little yellow flowers spread across the lush green. On a far rise, a house could be built where aspens and pines would shade the front porch, and he rode over to it. He reined up and twisted about for a view of the valley, but his stallion snorted and danced, and Cass spun it around.

"Darringer, what are you doing here?"

Coming out of the trees, leading his horse, was Ross Langdon, looking plenty mean and tough. Yet Cass was glad to see him.

"I was admirin' this place. What's it called?"

"Sweet Meadow."

"I wouldn't mind havin' it."

"It ain't for sale."

"I'm not here to fight with you, Mr. Langdon."

Cass leaned on the pommel of his saddle as his stallion pawed the damp grass. He had a lot of respect for this man. What Ross Langdon had done about the mustangs had showed honor. But Cass was also hurting, and his leg was numb. He slid down from the saddle and limped over to a rock to sit down.

"What's happened to you this time?" Langdon asked.

The air was pure and clean, the sun warm as the two men sat on the rocks. He told Ross how he had been shot at twice and finally got Jenks, but Ross wasn't surprised.

"Never did like that dude."

"I'd sure like to talk to the sheriff about it, but he's out after rustlers near Target."

"Ain't never gonna catch 'em, but if I was to make a guess, it's the Poagues, every time."

"From what I seen, you got cattle to spare."

"They didn't come easy," Ross said. "And every cow or steer out there, it's like a year of my life."

"Where you from, originally?"

"Illinois. I was eight when the Sacs, led by ole Black Hawk, raided our valley. He was plenty mad because settlers had killed an Indian that was carrying a flag of truce. That was back in '32. I was hid under a wagon, on the springs. Saw it all. And I ain't never forgot."

"But now you have a family and all of this."

"Maybe so. But there are times when I ride out here to get away from everything that I wonder if a man oughta be lookin' to heaven for somethin' more."

Cass studied him. He liked this man a lot and hoped that if he had known his father, he would have been like Ross Langdon. Tough, sincere, honest, and retrospective.

Cass told him about his own childhood, how he had run away and became involved with hardcases, until Shorty saved him, and how his friend had been murdered.

"But you're a man now, Cass. We gotta play the cards the way they're dealt."

"You trust the sheriff?"

"Yeah, I do. He don't like nobody, not even himself."

They talked about politics and President Hayes, the previous year's war with the Nez Perce, minstrel shows, how it was unlikely the railroad would ever get up to Montana Territory, and life in general.

At length, they stood up, stretching. Both tightened their horses' cinches, but by now, Cass's leg was so stiff, Ross had to push him up in the saddle before mounting his own horse. The stallion pawed the grass and tossed its head.

"You ain't like no gunfighter," Ross said. "You oughta do somethin' better with your life."

"I had wanted to start a horse ranch with Shorty."

"That's a fine stallion. I hope you get on with it."

They said farewell, riding in opposite directions.

While the men rode, deep in thought, Texas was riding north from town on her sorrel mare, a slicker behind her saddle. The wagon road led to Langdon's

Lost River Ranch, and by the time Ross was home, she was in sight of the buildings and corrals. Men were saddling up near the bunkhouse. Surprised to see her, Tully rode to meet her and tipped his hat.

He expressed sympathy about Joker and took her up to the house where Ross Langdon opened the door.

"Mr. Langdon, is Rex at home?" she asked. "He's been wanting me to go riding with him."

"He'll be around. Come on in."

He let her inside where his wife, puffy and weary, was bundled up in a chair by the hearth. She graciously greeted Texas and was glad for a woman's company.

Mrs. Langdon asked Texas everything about what women were doing and wearing, everywhere. She was curious about Texas' riding skirt.

"I made it," Texas said. "I sometimes rode with Joker and the freight wagons. You can't do that riding a one stirrup contraption, which I'm sure that a man invented."

Mrs. Langdon laughed. "I think you're right."

Ross sat watching his wife come to life. He was pleased, realizing how lonely for a woman's company his wife must be.

But when Mrs. Langdon went to lie down, Texas told Ross and his sons, who had just appeared, about Jenks's death.

"Never did like that man," Ross said. "I wonder what got into him?"

Later that afternoon, Rex and Texas went riding together. They crossed the hills and rode down to the shimmering river. He told her this would all be his someday. Dismounting, they sat on the rocks and gazed toward the white sandstone cliffs to the northeast where the Poagues lived.

Texas watched him as she spoke. "Why do you think Mr. Jenks tried to kill Cass."

Rex frowned. "Ain't for a girl to worry over."

"I don't understand what's going on, Rex."

"Texas, you shouldn't be worryin' so much."

"But Joker was killed. I have to know why."

He reached over and took her hand in his. "If I thought you were looking kindly on me, I'd find the answers for you."

"Would you, Rex?"

Beaming, he moved closer. She knew he wanted to kiss her, and it took all of her courage to remain seated.

"Texas, I've been most everywhere. Even all the way to New Orleans. But I ain't never seen anyone like you."

As he reached for her, she stopped him with a question that made him freeze and withdraw.

"Were you at the hanging?"

"I was out workin' cattle. Me and Rick."

"Do you know who the vigilantes were?"

"No, but I'll try and find out for you, if you gotta

know. Listen, you're not interested in Darringer, are you?''

''No, but he's been nice to me.''

''I'd like to be real nice to you, Texas.''

''Thank you,'' she said, rising quickly.

He stood up and caught her hand again. Sunlight was shining on her hair. She looked so beautiful, he swallowed hard. His face was turning all colors.

''Texas, I gotta ask you this. Right now.''

''What is it, Rex?''

''I wanta marry you.''

Startled, she stood frozen, staring at him. With great difficulty, she managed a smile and soft words.

''Rex, I'm honored you should ask me. But I'm not ready to marry anyone.''

''Will you think about it?''

''Yes, of course.''

He was satisfied. She carefully freed her hand and turned toward the horses, but abruptly, she stopped. Coming south along the river was a little old man on a mule. He was dirty and unkempt. Behind him trailed two pack burros, heavily loaded with gear.

''Simmons,'' Rex grunted. ''I seen him drooling over you whenever he's in town.''

''He's a good friend.''

''He ain't good for nothin'.''

Texas, however, was delighted to see the old man, waving him up the hill. He rode up to them, his eyes were almost hidden by his heavy grey brows, and he pushed his hat back as he glared at Rex, then grinned at her.

"Miss Texas, I didn't never expect to see you out here."

"Simmons, where you been?" Rex grunted. "You been diggin' up in them hills for years. Everyone else just stopped lookin'. Ain't no gold or silver up there. When are you gonna give up?"

"Ain't never gonna."

"Well, why don't you run along? Me and Miss Texas was busy talkin'."

The old man frowned. "You want me to leave, Miss Texas?"

"Mr. Simmons, if you're going back to town," she said, "I'd be pleased to ride along with you."

Rex was seriously annoyed. He walked Texas to her horse but she mounted without his offered assistance.

"Will you be sure to think about it?" Rex asked.

She nodded and turned her mount to join Simmons, who was back on his mule. As they rode south along the river toward town, the old man repeated his dream of riches.

"I'm gonna build you a real fancy house."

"What a nice idea," she said.

"You think I'm funnin' you, but you'll be surprised right soon."

She sadly told him about Thatcher's embezzlement and how Joker and Jenks had died.

Simmons was grim. "Well, I'm plannin' to stick around town awhile, look after you. I brought everything I owned down from the hills. Closed my camp for a time."

As they reached the town of Lost River, it was late afternoon. He insisted she go into Krutz's bank with him, and he led his packed burros right into the establishment.

The fat, bald, well-dressed banker jumped from behind his desk. Two proper ladies put their noses in the air and left in a hurry. Clerks backed away from the counters. One of the burros lifted its tail and deposited something of its own, right on the shining hardwood floor.

Krutz was horrified. "Simmons, get those animals outta here."

"Krutz, I got a deposit to make."

Texas and the banker stared as the old man took several heavy sacks from the burros, then sent the animals back outside with a clatter of hooves. He draped the dirty sacks over the banker's fancy desk.

"That there's gold, Krutz."

"You found gold? Where, man?"

"That's for me to know and you to wonder. Anytime I got a need, I can go back up and get some more. But

I got tired o' diggin'. So here's my dust and a few nuggets. Get to weighin'.''

"Sure, but we got no assay office here.''

"That's pure gold there. Just take a look.''

Sweating profusely, the banker stared at the contents of the bags. He weighed each sack of pure dust dotted with pure nuggets. When he was finished, he couldn't believe it. His eyes were round and opened wide.

"You got over thirty-five thousand here, Simmons.''

"Been diggin' and pannin' for years. Hit a glory hole. You open me an account for all but that one sack.''

Hands shaking, Krutz started filling out an account paper. Texas sat at Simmons side, proud of the little man and amazed. She had never seen so much gold, or so much wealth.

"Now,'' said Simmons, leaning over the desk. "I want my partner's name on there in case somethin' happens to me. You make sure she gets it.''

"Partner?'' Krutz asked.

"Texas Rafferty.''

Dumbfounded, Texas was in shock, and she stared as her full name was being entered on the bank's books with Simmons.

"Please,'' she said at length, "I can't let you do that.''

"You got nothin' to say about it,'' Simmons said.

"And I got no kin no how. And we're gonna be talkin' about me investin' in your freight line."

While she was signing with numb fingers, Krutz was agitated and squirming in his chair. Texas was going to be a rich young lady, and Krutz turned a framed picture around on his desk. It was the face of a handsome young man.

"My son," the banker told her. "He's on his way here for a visit."

"She don't want no dude," Simmons said. "And you keep your eyes off that gold. Me and Texas, we got our own plans."

Texas was still in shock as she followed Simmons outside. Sack of dust in hand, Simmons turned to see Bucky and Cass approaching. Bucky was drafted to take care of the mule and burros for a small but solid gold nugget.

Cass was curious, but he didn't say much as Texas asked him to go with them to the freight office. He limped along with them, his leg still hurting, and he was startled as Simmons plunked the gold bag on the counter.

"Now you get them papers out, Texas, honey, and we're gonna put my name along side yours, and we'll make our mark so it's legal, and Cass can witness. Your Pa's outfit is gonna be the biggest in these parts. Now put this here sack in your safe."

"Later, she turned, hugged him and gave him a big

kiss. When the red-faced Simmons had gone to his shack, she and Cass sat down over coffee, and she told him what had happened at the bank.

"Don't tell anyone else," he said.

The next day, Simmons gave money to repair the town hall, and everyone pitched in to get ready for the first town dance in over a year. Everyone was excited. Word had been sent to most of the ranchers.

Simmons had taken over the operation of the freight line, and with his investment, they were buying more mules and wagons, along with hiring more mule skinners. He was already making deals with merchants in Butte.

The afternoon before the dance, Cass was crossing the street when he paused at the thunder of hooves. He turned in time to see five horses bearing down on him. He spun and leaped backward, landing on his feet.

The Poagues, dirty, unkempt, laughing, reined up to look down at him. Rufus was apparently the oldest and the leader, still wearing his fancy spurs. They were all bearded giants. They sure didn't look like ranchers, none of them. They were some ancient breed.

"Darringer, can't you see where you're goin'?" Rufus asked.

"Reckon not," Cass said.

"Well, now, we been hearin' stories about you shootin' down some more of our fine citizens. You hexed?"

"Does that worry you?"

"I just figure anytime I wanta get rid of you, all I gotta do is mash you into a pulp. But we come for the big dance tonight and ain't got time for you."

"Remember," Cass said. "No spurs. No liquor. No tobacco spittin'. And you have to take a bath."

The Poagues thought this was very funny and had a hearty laugh, then rode on toward the livery.

Back at the rooming house to clean up for the dance, he was stopped by Celia who asked if he was escorting Texas, because she wanted to go with them.

Cass had to find out the answer for himself, and he went outside and across to the freight office. Simmons and Texas were inside, and Simmons was combing his thin hair.

Texas was wearing a frilly green dress, and she had her red hair in great waves about her pretty face. She turned to look at Cass, who had lost his voice as he stared at her.

"Oh, here he is now, Mr. Simmons. My escort."

Simmons looked Cass over and made a face. "Well, you have any problems, you holler. I'll be over at the town hall. But I reckon I won't worry too much. He's got so many bullet holes in 'im, all the hot air's probably blown away."

"Oh, Cass, that's right. Are you sure you can dance?"

"All I can do is try."

The old man left, and Cass turned to look at Texas with a mixture of anticipation and dread. He wanted to be around her, close to her, and he wanted to dance with her, but he was right scared.

She smiled, smoothing her gown. "How do I look?"

"Uh, right nice."

"You were planning to escort me, weren't you?"

"Yeah, uh, you and Miss Celia both."

She frowned. "Celia?"

"She's crazy about Tully, but he ain't here."

With a relieved smile, she took up her heavy shawl. "Shall we go find her then?"

She took his arm, and his face was burning as he led her across the street to the rooming house. She went inside to find Celia.

He waited on the boardwalk in the cold, the stars bright and close, the moon giving wondrous light. Up the street, a lot of cowboys were already joining local townspeople who were milling outside the hall, waiting for it to open.

He could see the Langdons and their men up the street, and Tully left them to walk down to where Cass was standing. Tully was clean as a whistle and even smelled like soap, his hair slicked back, and he was wearing a new red shirt.

"Cass, you gotta help me. Now Silvers, he told me what I got to say to a lady and all, but I might forget. You gonna help me out?"

"I'm not so good at that myself."

"I mean I gotta ask her to dance."

"Celia?"

"Yeah, but I'm scared silly."

"She wants you to escort her to the dance."

Tully was a sudden shambles, and when Celia came out the door, he turned several shades of red. She looked pretty in a dark blue dress and cape. Smiling as she studied Tully, causing him to fidget, she turned to Cass.

"You've found help, Cass? Were you afraid to be alone with two ladies?"

"Oh, I was just passin' by" Tully said, frantic.

"He wants to apologize," Cass said.

Tully turned white. "Uh—"

"What he's tryin' to say," Cass told her, "is that he's mighty sorry he grabbed you that day. He's not much good around real ladies. And you were so pretty, he just couldn't help himself."

Now Tully was dark red. "Uh—"

"And," Cass continued, "he'd be powerful glad if you would allow him to escort you to the dance."

Celia saw a dismayed Tully before her. The man was a complete disaster, shaking all over, and it pleased her. She smiled and took his arm, and he nearly fell over from sheer delight.

"I think that's a nice idea," she said.

Mrs. Barnes, wearing black, came outside and

frowned at the foursome, and walked along with them. Texas took Cass's arm, and he felt right proud.

The dance was a huge success. The hall was pretty with paper flowers, decorations and lace curtains at the windows. No one balked at the entrance fee. There were no fights, and the music was grand.

Simmons hung on Texas's every word and danced with her more than once. The respectable ladies of the town fawned over her, knowing she had become very wealthy.

Tully managed somehow to dance with Celia. She helped him find the right steps. He was clumsy, tongue-tied, red-faced and embarrassed. Rick constantly cut in, and Tully returned the favor.

It was Rex Langdon who was furious when Texas turned him down for the first dance. He had to stand back and watch as she moved into Cass's arms.

Cass's leg was still stiff and bandaged, and his shoulder hurt, but when he put his arm about her, he forgot everything but the fire in her hair and the sky-blue of her large eyes.

They swayed to a smooth waltz, and he felt no pain. She smiled up at him as if he was the only man in the world, and she felt soft and supple in his embrace. He thought of her kiss at the picnic, and his face turned hot.

"Cass, are you sure you're all right?"

"Uh, it's just a little warm in here."

It was then that an angry Rex cut in and tried to monopolize her the rest of the evening. Cass was hurting, so he forced himself to sit with Ross and savor the punch.

"My wife insisted I come," the rancher said, "so I could tell her all about it. She's been gettin' better though, since the doctor told her she can't have no sugar."

"You're a lucky man, Mr. Langdon."

Ross nodded, but he frowned as he watched his sons. When the dance was over, it was three in the morning. The happy townspeople filed out into the cold night.

Cass and Tully walked the women home. There were too many onlookers for either one to consider stealing a kiss.

Tully was a happy man when he rode out of town with the other Langdon hands. The rancher and Rick rode with them, but there was no sign of Rex.

Cass stood outside the rooming house, too wide awake to enter. He leaned on a post and gazed at the stars. He missed being out there at night, for it was a lot easier to talk to the Lord with no roof in the way.

He suddenly stiffened, hearing strange sounds from across the lot that separated the rooming house and the dancehall, behind which Simmons had his shack. Noises. Like pounding on sacks. Heavy breathing. Mumbled voices.

He moved around the rooming house and turned

quietly into the lot. Behind that building and next to Simmons's shack, a scuffle was going on. A fight. He saw a shadowy figure kicking something on the ground.

Cass drew his six-gun and moved closer as he heard a muffled voice.

"Darn you, Simmons, where'd you get the gold?"

Turning the corner, Cass paused. Rex Langdon, rifle in hand, was standing over Simmons, who lay on the ground and looked badly hurt, trying to shield his face with his arms.

"Talk, blast you."

Before Cass could move, Langdon hit Simmons on the side of the head with the butt of his rifle. There was a loud crack.

Cass stepped forward. "Hold it."

Chapter Seven

Rex turned his rifle on Cass. "Get outta here."

"Leave that old man alone."

"He found gold out there. Been hidin' and hoggin' it all these years. Maybe he even dug it off our land."

Abruptly, the back window of the dancehall opened, light falling on Rex and Cass. It was Swaps, the bartender.

"What's goin' on out there?"

"Better call the doctor," Cass said. "Simmons is hurt."

Swaps backed away, and Rex ignored him as he kept his rifle aimed at Cass and growled.

"That old man ain't hurt much. Ain't my fault he won't talk."

"I'm locking you up."

"You wanta make this a showdown?" Rex taunted. "You want to draw against this rifle? Go ahead, Darringer. I'll blow you apart before you slap leather."

Suddenly, Swaps charged into Rex, throwing him off balance, the rifle swinging upward. Furious, Rex shoved him away, then grazed him across the forehead with the butt.

At the same moment, Cass rushed in, seizing the rifle. They struggled for it, straining against each other, breathing hard as each used every muscle to overpower the other.

Cass jerked the rifle downward, the butt crammed hard in Rex's middle. With a gasp, Rex doubled up in agony. Cass leaped backward and free, aiming the rifle at him.

"All right, Langdon. Let's go."

Rex was fighting for breath, gazing up at him with wild eyes. Gasping, he tried to pull his sixgun, but with the butt of the rifle, Cass knocked it out of his hand. Rex couldn't straighten up, and he was trying to talk but couldn't.

"Get the doctor," Cass said.

Swaps went off like a shot, and he soon had the doctor running over to Cass, who then marched Rex off toward the jail.

"My Pa will get you for this, Darringer."

"I'm lockin' you up 'til the sheriff gets back."

"Well, he'll just let me out again. So I'll just have some sleep while I'm waitin'. And I won't have to ride all day."

"Get movin'."

With a sneer, Rex walked across the lot and onto the boardwalk. The town was asleep as Cass marched him all the way to the sheriff's office. The door, as usual, was unlocked. Inside, a lantern still burned low in the corner. Cass reached over and turned it up.

After he had locked Rex in the cell, Cass sat down at the desk and wrote a long explanation to the sheriff. He hung the keys on his belt. Then he stood up and looked back toward Rex Langdon. The man was already stretched out on a cot.

Moving outside, Cass felt again the chill of night. He walked back along the boardwalk. As he reached the empty lot, he hurried to join the doctor and bartender where they knelt by Simmons.

The doctor stood up slowly. "He's dead."

Swaps was in tears. "Them Langdons oughta not get away with this."

"You willing to testify?"

"Well, sure. Ain't no way Langdon can say old Simmons just fell down and hit his head. And you seen Rex do it. And he as much admitted it right in front of me."

"That's right."

"But Ross Langdon runs this town and the whole valley. Rex is gonna be turned loose."

"Not if I can help it."

They said goodnight. Weary, Cass started to cross over to the rooming house, but he saw lights in the freight office, and there was Texas in the doorway in a blue wrapper, looking around frantically, rifle in hand. He walked over to her and removed his hat, running his hand over his sweaty hair.

"Cass, what's going on? I heard a lot of noise outside. And voices."

"Rex beat Simmons to death, trying to find out where his mine is. Must of caught him by surprise, because Simmons never had a chance to call for help. I put Rex in jail."

Tears filled her eyes. "Dear God."

She stumbled forward and into his arms. He held her as she sobbed her grief for Simmons. At length, she drew back in his arms, her face wet.

"First my father, then my uncle, and now poor Mr. Simmons. And it's not over. They'll never let you hold Rex."

"In the morning, go to Joe's Cafe and have them send breakfast over. When's the circuit judge coming?"

"I don't know."

She gazed at him with great distress, then, as the tears trickled down her face, she went back into the office, closing the door behind her.

The bank account Simmons had opened would be hers now, though it had not yet crossed her mind. She would no longer have to run the freight company.

In his room, Cass gathered his gear and a change of clothes and went downstairs without a sound.

Down at the jail, Rex was snoring in his cell. Cass

barred the door and shuttered the two front windows. Then he lay on the lawman's cot and gazed at the ceiling in the pale lamplight. A bug was crawling up there. He lay staring at it with no thought of killing it. Life was too precious, too easily cut short. He was sick of death.

He awakened at dawn. It was Saturday. He slid aside a shutter on the left front window, peering outside.

It was a sunny day. There were a lot of wagons in town for supplies. Children played over by Joe's Cafe. Women were gathered in a group nearby, whispering, most likely about Simmons. He saw no sign of the Langdons.

Rex was up and gripping the bars with both hands.

"You'd better let me out of here, Darringer. My Pa will tear this place apart. And you with it."

"You beat an old man to death."

"The old fool died?"

"I saw you do it. You're gonna hang."

"My word against yours. Who's gonna take a gun-fighter's word against a Langdon's?"

"Swaps saw it."

"He didn't see nothin'. You're wastin' your time, Darringer. I'm gettin' off free and you know it."

"You're standin' trial just the same."

"Listen to me, Darringer. You're a dead man, one way or the other."

It was noon before there was a knock at the door.

Tully called out, and Cass peered out the window to see that the cowhand was alone before letting him inside.

Rex jumped up. "Where's my Pa?"

Tully looked uneasy. "He's down at the livery with the men. He sent me ahead to try to talk sense to Cass. He don't want no killin'."

Cass led Tully outside, closing the door behind them. He looked down the street toward the livery but saw no sign of the Langdons. He turned to the cowhand, who was nervous and speaking in whispers.

"Cass, you're really in trouble. Ross has his son Rick and a dozen men with him. Did you really see Rex kill Simmons?"

"Yes, I did."

Tully was agitated. "I don't wanna see you get killed. Why don't you let him out? Then the sheriff can arrest him again when he comes back."

"I can't do that, Tully. I saw that poor old man die."

"I thought you was here because of your partner bein' killed."

"That's why I'm here all right, and I don't trust nobody. I figure Webb didn't arrest the vigilantes because his nephew was one of them. And maybe he knows who the others are. For all I know, Langdon's sons were both at the hangin'. But right now, I want justice for Simmons, an old man who never did harm to anyone.''

''So what do I tell Mr. Langdon?''

''His son stays in jail.''

''You can't hold 'em off, Cass.''

''I'm sure gonna try.''

Tully was unhappy and turned away. Cass went back inside and barred the door. Rex was gripping the bars, his face all colors.

''Blast you, Darringer. Where's my Pa?''

''He's comin' to break you out of here.''

''About time.''

Cass took down the shotgun from the rack, checking the load in both barrels. Then he went to the front window on his left and slid the shutter aside a few inches.

Langdon, his son Rick and a dozen men, along with Tully, were gathering out front on foot. Silvers was among them but standing off to one side.

''Darringer,'' the rancher called. ''I wanna talk.''

Cass opened the door and stood aside with the shotgun visible. ''Leave your guns and come in alone.''

Carefully, Cass allowed the unarmed rancher to enter. He closed the door and barred it with one hand, keeping the shotgun leveled.

Ross Langdon walked over to the cell where Rex was gripping the bars with both hands, his face ashen and eyes round in anguish.

"Pa, you gotta get me outta here."

"Don't worry, son. He's got no authority."

"I have a citizen's authority," Cass corrected. "And I saw him kill Simmons."

"Rex, did you kill that old man?"

"No, Pa. You got no right to even ask that. I found him all beat up. Then Darringer comes along and says I done it. Maybe it was him, Pa. Maybe Darringer done it."

Ross slumped a little. "I was talkin' with Swaps."

"He didn't see nothin', Pa."

The rancher turned slowly. "Darringer, if you'll turn him loose, I'll make sure he's available for trial."

"It's up to the sheriff."

Rex was frantic. "Pa, I didn't do nothin'. I ain't standin' for no trial."

"The sheriff may not be back for days," Ross said.

"Your son will be well fed. And he won't be hurt."

Langdon was grim. "A lot of people liked ole Simmons. And they ain't too fond of the Langdons. If they get hot about the killin' and blame my son, there could be a lynchin'."

"They'd have to get past me."

"I'll give you some of my men."

"No, thanks."

"Why are you mixin' in this, Darringer?"

"Like you said. A lot of people liked ole Simmons."

"Hey, Pa, maybe that woman did it. Texas. With

him dead, she gets it all, Pa. That's reason enough, eh?''

''She's just a young girl,'' Ross said.

Rex was shaking the bars with his grip. ''Pa, just get me out o' here.''

''When the sheriff comes back,'' the rancher said, walking to the door. ''Maybe he'll figure there's not enough evidence to hold you.''

''Pa, come back.''

''We'll be around, son. We ain't gonna let anyone near you.''

Cass spoke abruptly. ''You got one man I'd trust to help me out. Send Tully over.''

''He's yours. He'll be right in.''

Rex relaxed a little, certain he could handle the ignorant Tully. The rancher left, and soon Tully came to the door. When Cass let him inside, the cowhand looked plenty nervous.

''I just need help when I have to get out o' here,'' Cass said, ''or while I'm sleepin'.''

Tully shrugged. ''Well, sure.''

But when Cass left the jail to attend Simmons's funeral at mid-afternoon, he took the keys with him. Tully sat at the desk while Rex glared at him.

''Blast it, Tully, you gotta get me outta here.''

''I can't do nothin'. Cass has got the keys.''

''You work for me, Tully. You gotta do somethin'.''

''I work for Mr. Langdon.''

"And me, and Rick. Ain't you got no sense?"

"Not much, and right now, I'm mighty sleepy."

Tully put his feet on the desk and promptly fell asleep.

While he slept and Rex fumed, a funeral was held for Simmons up near the church. Afterward, Cass walked Texas to the door of the freight office.

"Cass, I'm worried about you."

"No need. That jail's like a fortress."

"But don't you realize the men who've been trying to kill you will see this as an opportunity? They could work up a mob to get at Rex, then let him go when you're dead."

"Maybe."

"Can't you let him free until the sheriff returns?"

"No."

"You're a stubborn man, Cass Darringer."

With the back of his big hand, he touched her flushed, hot cheeks. "But are you all right?"

"I'm terribly sad. And I've had four proposals of marriage already this morning. They all know about the gold."

"It ain't just the gold they want."

Suddenly, there was a loud voice from behind them. "Cass Darringer!"

They turned to look at Silvers across the street. He had come out of the general store and was standing on the boardwalk with his hands at his sides. Tall, lean of body and face, loose skin around his eyes, a rolled smoke dangling from his thin lips, the man was challenging him.

Texas was frightened. "Cass, please, no. This is what Langdon wants."

Cass felt his mouth go dry. He knew that Silvers was an experienced gunman and was cold, calculating, unafraid. This was no Arizona Kid. This man was a killer of men with no regrets, a man who could shoot anyone down and then have his supper and enjoy it.

Silvers stepped slowly into the street. Cass moved along the boardwalk, away from Texas, his back to the alley between the freight office and the nearest saloon. His heart was thumping like crazy, but he stepped down into the dry mud.

"You know what I want," Silvers said.

"Langdon payin' you for this?"

"This one's for free, Darringer."

"I got no call to fight you."

Silvers raised his voice. "You rode with the Red River gang. You took three men down in Socorro. Only one of 'em got his six-shooter clear of the holster."

"Ain't got nothin' to do with you."

"You're wrong, Darringer. My name's gonna be a lot bigger when I take you down."

The gunman moved a few more steps, bringing him within twenty feet. Cass felt the weight of his Colt in his holster. His hands felt damp. Sweat was on his brow and trickling down his back. He could feel his heart beating crazy in his chest. His breath was short.

He knew Texas was watching. Others were appearing on the far edges of the street. Some retreated to windows and doors.

The two men faced each other in careful silence.

The Poages had joined the crowd now, but there was no sign of the Langdons. Silvers didn't seem to mind the audience, but this was business with him. His voice was chilling.

"We both knew it would come to this."

"I don't have to prove anything, Silvers. Why don't you just walk away?"

"Can't do that."

They stood watching each other, waiting. Neither wanted to draw first. Using his left hand, Silvers pulled out a silver dollar, holding it up in the sunlight.

"When this hits the ground, Darringer, you'd better draw."

Chapter Eight

The silver dollar went sailing into the air. The town held its breath. The sun caught the gleam as it seemed to hesitate, then came plunging back down to earth. When it hit, both men drew and fired. The shots echoed, loud and clear, the smell of gunpowder lingering.

Cass was hit on the left ear lobe, and it burned. Silvers was slowly dropping to his knees, blood on his chest, dead center. He was staring at Cass in disbelief, his reputation lost, his life ebbing away even as he tried to lift his Colt for one last shot.

Then Silvers managed to smile as he swayed. In his last breath, he was trying to die with bravado—there was no fear in his darkening gaze. Slowly, painfully, he crumpled up and fell twisted and dead on the ground.

Cass realized he had been holding his breath, and he couldn't believe he was still alive. He put his left hand to his bleeding ear and looked at the Poagues. Then he saw the Langdons down the street on the far boardwalk past the jail, near the gunsmith. He started for the jail, but Texas hurried into the street to catch his arm.

"Cass, let me help you. I can fire a rifle."

"Could you kill a man?"

"Yes."

He shook his head. "It ain't easy, and I don't want you dreamin' about it for the rest of your life."

"Do you dream about it?" she whispered.

"Always."

Cass turned away from her and the milling crowd.

When he reached the jail, Tully let him inside. Cass let him help clean his wounded ear as he told him what had happened with Silvers, while Rex sat brooding and listening.

Tully was nervous. "There's gonna be trouble."

"You can leave."

"Ain't right, you here by yourself."

Rex pounded the bars. "Get out o' here, Tully."

Tully shrugged, suddenly making up his mind. "I ain't leavin' 'til the sheriff comes back. That's what Mr. Langdon said."

"Blast you, Tully!" Rex bellowed.

Tully's swarthy face was darker now as he realized what course he had taken. Cass went back to the desk, and Tully sat in front of it, settling in the chair with sudden exhaustion. Then he laughed at his own foolishness.

"Tully," Rex growled, "you're a fool."

"Reckon so," Tully said.

Snarling, Rex sat back down in his cell. Tully was sweating, but his mind was set, and he took up a deck of cards, shuffling them over and over. He and Cass played a few hands of poker as night fell.

Soon there was a knock at the door. It was food and a jug of water brought by the old man from Joe's Cafe. Texas was carrying the coffee kettle and set it on the iron stove. Celia followed with the extra cups and another jug of water.

As the old man left, Texas and Celia stood firm.

"Get out of here," Cass said, towering over them.

Texas tried to stand taller. "I can shoot as good as any man. I'm staying."

Cass grimaced. "If they come at us, an army couldn't hold 'em off. You'll just get hurt."

"You said this place was a fortress."

Rex was at the bars, fists grabbing them. "Texas, honey, tell 'em to let me out of here."

Celia was looking up at Tully, her smile hesitant. "You're very brave to stay in here, Mr. Tully."

The cowhand's face turned pink as he blushed. She came closer, reaching up to touch his grizzled cheek. He nearly died from joy.

Cass took the arms of both women and marched them to the door. When they were gone, he shook his head in disbelief.

Late that night, Cass left Tully in charge while he

went out to check the town. He knew he could be a target, but he didn't like being holed up like a rat. Near the last saloon, Cass paused to listen away from the swinging doors.

"Men," Rufus Poague was saying, "it ain't right that a gunfighter's sittin' in there pretendin' to be sheriff. And he's locked up ole Rex for somethin' he didn't do."

"Yeah," said another Poague, "that Darringer is lyin' through his teeth, all right."

Cass peered through the window into the smoke-filled room. The dirty, unkempt Poagues were gathered at the bar. They had the attention of some of the cowhands. The others were too busy playing cards.

"You can't get in there," the bartender said to Rufus. "It's like a fort. Them walls are plenty thick."

"Not too thick for dynamite," a little man with spectacles said.

"Yeah, Bixby," said Rufus, "you know about that stuff. We'll need you. Seems to me, we oughta bust ole Rex out. Then we oughta just hang that Darringer. He's already killed five men. Poor Arizona, he was just a kid. And Thatcher, sittin' at his desk, nice as can be. And Jenks. And poor Simmons. And now Silvers, shot dead in the street. Men, we can't just sit around and let that gunfighter run our town."

Back inside the jail, Cass sat down at the desk. Tully was nervous but determined to stay. He sat down facing

Cass. Rex was snoring in his cell, one arm dangling from the cot.

"Look bad?" Tully asked, leaning back in his chair.

"Poagues are stirrin' things up, all right. Seems like it's me they want, not Rex. Where would they get dynamite?"

"Barnes's store, most likely. Except for Simmons, folks gave up on prospectin' around here a long time ago. So it'd be plenty old and right dangerous to fool with."

"Who's Bixby?"

"Worked for the railroad and did some mining. Yeah, he'd know about dynamite, all right."

"Tully, you think Langdon set Silvers on me?"

"No. Silvers was one of Rex's hires. So was Arizona. Mr. Langdon would do his own fightin'."

"You think Ross'd join the Poagues in gettin' Rex out?"

"He don't like the Poagues much. He thinks they been rustlin' his cattle. He might just sit back and watch. But he won't want Rex hurt."

"If they come at us with dynamite, they'll hit the front to avoid gettin' Rex."

"What you figure we oughta do?"

Cass sat quiet, his thoughts churning. The walls were plenty thick. The vulnerable spots were the two windows with the one inch shutters. The only heavy furniture in the room was the desk. It would only cover one window. It would also just go sliding across the room if the window was blown.

While Cass and Tully were thinking over their problem, Ross Langdon and his son Rick were at the hotel on the hill. They sat alone in what had once been a plush lobby. Rick was nervous.

"Maybe I oughta go see what's happenin', Pa."

"You stay out of it."

"You just gonna sit there and wait for the sheriff? Don't you care about your own son?"

"I care enough not to tell Webb you and Rex was at that lynchin'. But don't push me too far, Rick."

Before Rick could answer, Rufus Poague came charging in like a grizzly. Panting, he plunked his dirty frame down in a soft green chair that swayed under his weight.

"All right, Langdon. This is it. We got the town pretty stirred up against Darringer. And we're gettin' some dynamite."

"What? You'll get Rex killed."

"No, we got us Bixby. He knows how to handle it. We're just gonna open the front, that's all."

"Rufus, no dynamite."

"Darringer ain't gonna give up 'til he finds out who was at the hangin' and killed his partner. None of us is gonna be safe. Not me and my kin or your two boys."

"Wait for the sheriff, Rufus."

"I'm not trustin' anything to Webb. And you shouldn't either. Jenks was at the hangin' and when he was dyin', he was alone with the sheriff and probably told him everything. Webb will hang us all, includin' your sons."

"Hold on," Ross said, "you mean Jenks was at the hangin', too?"

"Yeah, Jenks and Barnes, your boys, and Bixby. And me and my cousins. In fact, it was ole Rex who shot Darringer out of the saddle. Course we didn't know who he was then."

Ross glared at his son. "So all you did was watch."

"Pa, wasn't Rex payin' the sheriff?"

"He wouldn't take it," Rufus said, standing up slowly. "Listen to me, Ross. We're bustin' in that jail tonight to get Rex out. And we'll take care of Darringer."

Ross was pale, leaning back in his chair. "No, Rufus."

"Pa, you want your sons to hang?"

"This has got to stop. The old days are gone."

Rufus walked over to the door. "Listen, Ross, if you ain't comin' to help out, then you stay here and keep out o' it. We'll send ole Rex right to you."

Abruptly, Bixby, a wiry little man, stuck his head in the door. "Rufus, the sheriff's ridin' into town."

"All right then," said Rufus, sneering. "We get

'em both. Cass Darringer and the sheriff. When they're gone, no one will know we was at the hangin'."

"Each one of you will know," Ross said. "You gonna kill each other off?"

"The vigilantes swore an oath of silence," Rufus said.

"So who killed Barnes?"

"Oh, that," said Rufus. "He was gettin' too scared, on account of he thought maybe Darringer had seen his face when he was up there kickin' him. Ole Barnes was tryin' real hard to be a man, but he started fallin' apart. So Jenks took care of 'im."

Ross was nauseated. "You listen to me, Rufus. No dynamite. Or I'll blow your brains out. And we're waitin' for the sheriff."

"Have it your way, Langdon."

The giant and the little man left. The room smelled from their sweat, and Ross Langdon felt sick in his gut. His valley, this town, his sons, all gone bad. He liked Cass Darringer and didn't want him hurt, but Rex was his son. He felt like he was trapped in a vice.

Rick was anxious. "Pa, ain't you gonna help out?"

"What was your part in this?"

"Nothin', Pa. I just went along for the ride."

Later that night, with Rex snoring in his cell, Cass opened the door for Sheriff Webb, who came out of the darkness and into the lamplight with dismay on his bearded face. Barring the door, Cass turned to watch the weary, dust covered lawman stare at the cell where Rex was snoring. Tully was pouring coffee and yawning.

"They told me at the livery what was goin' on," the sheriff said. "I didn't believe it."

"My question is," said Cass, "just how much do you know, sheriff? For instance, what about Jenks? He tried to kill me twice. He had to have a good reason."

"I got plenty to say about that. After I have some coffee."

The sheriff sat down at his desk, tired and worn. He told them he'd been tracking rustlers and lost them.

"Ain't slept," the lawman said.

"Tully," Cass said, "maybe you oughta get outta here now that the sheriff's back."

Looking insulted, Tully shook his head. "I'm stayin'."

"We have to wait for the circuit judge," the lawman said. "I sent for help from Deer Lodge, but it may not get here in time."

They settled around the desk and were sharing old coffee when they heard a rumble in the street. The sheriff stood up and moved a shutter aside. There was a mob all right. More than sixty men with torches. Cass turned down the lamps.

"Sheriff, you let Rex go," Rufus shouted.

Taking up his shotgun, the sheriff unbarred the door and kept to the side of the doorway. Tully and Cass stayed out of sight. The sheriff carefully leaned forward.

"Rufus, you and these men go on back to the saloon."

"Rex didn't kill Simmons. That Darringer done it and we aim to hang 'em. He's killed five men now. Poor Arizona, ole Thatcher, your nephew, and Simmons and now Silvers. And maybe he got ole Barnes."

"My nephew killed Barnes. And Rex is gonna stand trial. You want Montana to be a state? Or you want it to be a place where vigilantes run everything?"

"Just give us Darringer," Rufus growled.

"No," the lawman said. "He ain't done nothin' but act in self defense. Now get outta here, Rufus, or you're the first one'll get this shotgun in the face."

The mob began moving back, torches still burning. The sheriff closed the door and barred it, and he was so weary, he had to force himself back to his chair.

"They leavin'?" Tully asked.

"Just to get the dynamite," Cass said.

Settling down at the desk, the sheriff looked worn to the bone. Rex, who had been awakened by the mob, was grinning from ear to ear. He demanded to be let out, but Webb ignored him, and soon Rex was snoring away in his cell.

Webb toyed with the keys Cass had returned to him.

"Sit down, Darringer. I got somethin' to say."

Cass and Tully sat in front of the desk, waiting. The lawman cleared his throat and spoke grimly.

"When my nephew was dying, I was alone with him. He said he was one of the vigilantes. So was Barnes, who was about to confess afore my nephew got him. And Bixby, the five Poagues and the Langdon boys. Soon's help gets here from Deer Lodge, I'll be makin' some arrests."

"Even old Barnes," Tully said, shaking his head.

"Who shot me out of the saddle?" Cass asked.

Webb nodded to the cell. "Rex."

"And Jenks told you all this?"

"Sure did," the lawman said. "He was brought up in the church. He wanted a clean slate."

Cass tightened his hands around his cup. "And who killed Shorty? And Joker?"

"That I don't know. He died afore it all got out."

"Poor old Jenks," Tully said. "He was a real dude."

The lawman shrugged. "What I heard from Jenks'll be admitted, all right. They don't figure a man would die with a lie on his lips. And he sure ain't available for trial."

"What's more," Cass said, "you tellin' about your own nephew like that, they got to believe it's true."

Webb turned to Tully. "No need for you to be here. It's me and Darringer they want dead. And maybe you can get Ross Langdon to back off."

Tully shook his head. "Langdon won't listen to anyone with his son in here. Maybe he won't be with the others, but he won't stop 'em. He wants Rex out. And I'm stayin'."

"So that's it," the sheriff said.

The three men looked at the windows. They knew a dynamite blast could blow them right back to the cells. By morning, the three of them could be dead, their bodies scattered in a lot of pieces. It was something to think about.

"All my fault," Cass said, cold and bitter. "If I hadn't come to Lost River, none of this would have happened."

"You did what you had to do," Webb told him.

Cass and Tully moved over to the chairs by the stove and began to play checkers. Neither could sleep, nor could they concentrate. The lawman slept on his bunk, exhausted, and Rex was still snoring, arms and legs dangling from the cot.

Around midnight, Sheriff Webb suddenly sat up, eyes wide open, and he got up to turn down the lamps.

Tully and Cass, dozing in their chairs, looked up slowly. The lawman went to a window, sliding the shutter a crack. His senses were reeling. He saw nothing in the moonlight, but he was plenty nervous. He closed the window, put his big hand over the lamps to kill the flames, and picked up his shotgun.

"Get in that other cell. Quick."

They hurried behind the bars of the empty cell, feeling foolish but anxious. Tully ran his fingers through his hair. Cass rested his hand on his Colt as tension gripped them. The lawman stood by the cell door, gripping a bar and listening.

"I don't hear anything," Tully murmured.

Chapter Nine

Suddenly, a deafening explosion sent half of the front wall hurtling toward them. Wood and glass and chairs and the stove chimney and half the roof were carried with it, crashing and slamming against the bars as the men fell back to the floor, stunned. Rex was knocked off his cot like a feather.

The impact stayed a long moment, dust and debris settling down against the bars with a clatter. Half of the front of the roof was gone, replaced by moonlight. The front door and a portion of the wall near the desk were still standing under a partial roof which extended to cover the cells. The rest of the jail to their right was gone.

"Wow," Rex said, getting up off the floor.

The three men in the other cell shoved the door open against the debris. Armed with his shotgun, Sheriff Webb stumbled over the boards and debris and worked his way over to the open space around his desk.

Cass and Tully, six-guns in hand, made their way forward, falling more than once, to join him behind the remaining wall. They saw no movement in the street. Turning the desk on its side on top of the rubble, they used it for a side wall. The cells had a roof but no protection from the front, except the fallen debris.

"Dadburn it," a rough voice said from the night.

"They ain't dead," another said.

"You want more?" Rufus shouted.

Webb shouted back. "Go ahead. But if we die, so does Rex Langdon. You near killed him."

They heard muffled arguments. Abruptly, there was silence. The three men in what was left of the jail took turns sitting down in the remaining chairs to recover.

"Next time they use dynamite," said Tully, "they'll get us."

Webb shook his head. "No, be too risky for Rex. They don't want Langdon mad at 'em. They'll try shootin', come mornin', on account of they can miss him easy enough."

While the three men waited and Rex sat nervously in a corner of his cell with nothing in front of him but bars, Rufus Poague was storming up the street like a locomotive. His cousins had scattered into alleys across from the jail, but he needed a drink.

Ross and Rick Langdon, half-dressed, were hurrying down the hill in the moonlight, and Rufus stopped as they came over to him. He held up his hand to ease the rancher's anger.

"Ross, don't worry. Rex is all right. But them other fellas is still alive, dadburn it."

Ross was furious. "I told you not to use dynamite. I oughta shoot you right now."

"Listen to me. We're gonna get Darringer and the sheriff outta there without takin' any more chances. No shootin' and no dynamite. I got me an idea. You and your boy get back to the hotel so you won't get no blame."

"I told you, Rufus. We're waitin' for the circuit judge, and I don't want any more of this. Come mornin', I'm going down to the jail to back 'em up."

"You'd do that?"

"I told you, I ain't lettin' you kill no lawman."

"Have it your way, Langdon. You're a fool."

Irate, Ross turned back up the hill with Rick.

Rufus stomped off up the dark street to join his four bearded kinfolk who had worked their way behind the buildings to the boardwalk. Two were sent to the livery for the horses. Rufus and the other two headed around back of the freight office. The building was dark, so they took down the lamp that hung outside the back door. Then they kicked the door open and stormed inside.

Dirty and unkempt, the Poagues charged into the hallway and into the back rooms. Rufus rushed into Texas's bedroom where she was still in bed in her nightgown but frantically reaching for a rifle in the pale lamplight. He knocked it out of her hand and slammed his fist into her jaw, snapping her head back, knocking her unconscious. He grabbed a silk scarf and tied it around her head and over her mouth.

Rufus saw her riding clothes draped over a chair. He grabbed them and her boots, then tossed them to a cousin. He picked her up as she started to come back to life, blankets and all, carrying her under his arm like a child, feet first. She clung to the bedpost. He jerked her free.

Near the door, she seized the water pitcher and twisted to crash it down on the side of his head, but missed. The vessel cracked and scattered in pieces. Rufus just laughed.

As they went out the back door, she fought, kicked and tried to scream but her cry was muffled by the scarf. He hit her again, and her head rolled to the side, unconscious. As he was throwing her across his saddle, Swaps came running out of the alley to stare, then back away.

Rufus snapped at him. ''You tell the sheriff we'll let her go just as soon as he and Darringer come out to our ranch. You tell 'em to come alone, and I mean alone, or we'll kill 'er.''

As they rode out of town, Swaps backed into the alley, turned and ran into the street. He crossed over to the jail and pounded on what was left of the door. Tully, half-asleep, stood up to see what was wrong and let him inside where Webb and Cass had been sleeping. Rex was pacing his cell, blanket around him, trying to see over the nearly five foot high, makeshift wall.

Swaps was out of breath. "Sheriff, they got Texas."

"What are you sayin'?"

"I heard somethin' back of the freight office and got worried about Texas and went to have a look. It was the Poagues. They took Texas. They said if you want her back, you and Cass Darringer gotta go to their ranch. Alone."

Webb was furious, pounding one fist into the other. Cass was drained down to his boots, barely able to stand.

"Don't worry, Darringer," the lawman said. "They won't hurt her. It's you and me they want dead."

"It'll be an ambush," Tully said, rubbing the sleep from his eyes. "You gotta go up Whiskey Gulch to get to their place. It'll be a trap, sure as shootin'. You won't have a chance."

Webb handed him the shotgun. "Tully, if Rex looks at you cross-eyed, you blow his head off. Swaps, come daylight, you find Ross Langdon and tell him what's happened. Poague thinks he won't care, but I don't figure Ross's gonna like it one bit."

Swaps left, and Tully sat down with the shotgun aimed across the desk wall at Rex, who was jubilant and shouting.

"This is how it ends, sheriff. You and Darringer.

You're gonna be dead. Then my Pa can just come and let me out.''

"He'll have to blast you out," Webb said, hooking the keys on his belt. "Let's go, Darringer."

The two men headed for the livery and saddled up. Webb took extra ropes and leather gloves, and they rode north out of town. It was still dark but the moonlight was clear. The lawman led the way down to the river. They forded the shallow water and turned northeast toward the distant white cliffs streaked with red.

"That's the way to Whiskey Gulch," Webb said. "Poagues are holed up behind them cliffs, and the canyon's the only way in. That's how it's hard to pin any rustlin' on 'em. Can't never find no cattle up there 'ceptin' their skinny herd. They got some way to sneak 'em out the back way to market, but I ain't found it."

Cass was still shaken. Texas in the hands of those unkempt, ugly, dirty giants. He pulled his hat down tight on his brow, his jaw set in anger. As cold as it was, his buckskin coat was too darned hot.

The sky was pale in the east. Soon it would be light. They followed a creek that led toward the cliffs. A raccoon hung high in one of the nearby lodgepole pines, peering down at them through its mask, eyes gleaming.

Ahead, Whiskey Gulch, a narrow, steep-walled canyon was waiting. Maples with new leaves lined part of the entrance. A tiny creek trickled through the pass.

Webb reined up. "They'll be waitin' to pick us off,

real easy. But with them ropes, maybe we can get over the wall.''

They rode west along the outside cliff for an hour. Finally, the sheriff reined to a halt, staring up at the steep wall. There were rocks jutting from the sandstone all the way up and on the rim. Still dangerous, but it was the lowest spot. They dismounted and began to ascend the cliff, using their hunting knives to carve handholds and trying to get their ropes up over the wall and onto one of the scrub junipers or a large rock.

While they were working on their climb, Texas was sitting in the ranch house with Rufus. It was a solid building with two rooms. The unkempt front room had a fireplace which was lit and hot. There was tarpaper on the walls. Several furs had been hung to add to the warmth. The furniture was mostly hand made. The other room, where she had been allowed to dress, was the cluttered bedroom with no windows, only rifle slits.

The only weapon in view was a Sharps buffalo rifle, hung above the mantle, where a box of cartridges was covered with dust. Sitting close to the hearth, warming her hands, she glanced carefully at Rufus. She didn't want to make the big man angry. With one hand, he could knock her across the room or strangle her.

''Don't worry,'' Rufus said, sitting in a big stuffed chair. ''It won't be long. My kinfolk are at the pass and can take care of Darringer and the sheriff and anyone else, real easy.''

"But if you kill the sheriff and Mr. Darringer, you'll be arrested."

"Who's gonna arrest me? Won't be no law around here. Besides, we was just defendin' ourselves. And we gotta close the books on a few things."

"You can't kill everyone in town."

"Listen to me. I'm gonna be the big he-bull around here when this is all over. And Rex, he's gonna be runnin' the Lost River Ranch. That's why I gotta save his hide."

"What are you saying?"

"Don't you listen? Rex, he's gonna get rid of his Pa, somehow. He tried to get Silvers to do it, but the fool wouldn't bite. So ole Rex, he's gonna do it hisself. Then we're all gonna be sittin' pretty."

She moved closer to the fire, distressed. If he was telling her all this, either he wasn't planning to let her go or he had some plans to keep her quiet for good.

"Rex and me, we work together. Why, whenever we needed some money, Rex and ole Rick would sneak some of their cattle over, and we'd take 'em through a wind tunnel in the back, and we'd sell 'em to one of the mining camps over by Target. Course we'd run the brands first."

"Rex was stealing his own cattle?"

"Well, makes sense, don't it? His Pa's a stingy man. That's why Rex made out a phony bill of sale for them mustangs. We split the money he got from the ranch safe.''

''You had the mustangs?''

''Yeah, we hanged them three fellas, but we really did figure they was guilty. When we got there, that old man tried to stop us. I took care of him right fast with my rifle butt, near busted his head off, and Rex was on guard and saw Darringer comin'. Didn't know who he was, so Rex shot him out of the saddle. Thought sure he was dead.''

She shivered. ''But why did you kill the mule and horses?''

''Didn't want 'em trailin' us or gettin' back afore we was safe. Darringer's horse got away. And then Darringer turns up alive. But we'll get him now. Him and Webb. Won't be no one left to do no talkin' about the lynchin'. We'll close the book on that, all right.''

Horrified, Texas stared into the fire, watching the flames dancing around the logs. Her heart was sick, knowing she was the bait.

''But now you ain't gonna be tellin' no one, I can promise you that,'' Rufus said. ''You're gonna marry Rex, and I know for a fact, you won't be able to say nothin' in court against your own man. Rex'll get that money ole Simmons left you, and we'll all be livin' high off the hog. But don't you worry. I ain't gonna hurt you. Ole Rex would have my hide.''

She wrapped her arms about herself. "Who killed Joker?"

"Rex, but he was aimin' at Darringer."

She glanced at the Sharps, then quickly concentrated on a picture frame on the mantle, also covered with dust. She wiped it off with her fingers and saw the face of an attractive, petite woman.

"Your wife?"

"Well, yeah, but she run off, went back to Ohio. Couldn't take it out here."

He went to the door, opening it, listening for gunfire. Disappointed, he closed the door and sat down, resting his rifle on his knee. He picked up a jug and began to take deep swallows of whiskey.

"Even if they get through Whiskey Gulch, they still won't get in the house. Not unless they want you dead."

While he rambled on, deeper intoxication slowly took hold of him. She cast her gaze around the room once more. The only available weapon was the Sharps. It was one big rifle.

If Rufus left the house, she could load it. If he got drunk enough, maybe she could get his Colt out of his holster. She had to do something, anything.

"Sit down," Rufus growled. "You make me nervous."

While Texas sat a prisoner, Cass and the sheriff made it over the cliff rim and crawled away from it, weary and out of breath. They rested in the warm sunlight, then got to their feet. Rifles and ropes in hand, they crossed the barren gravel and through the boulders and thick brush. When they reached the other side some three hundred yards across, they saw a deer trail heading down through the brush and rocks.

Further away in the small valley was a house. Nearby were corrals with horses. Some fifty scrub cattle grazed to the left. There were scattered trees and brush on the flat, but not enough cover.

"If we wait until night," the lawman said, "the Poagues in the canyon may get worried. Some of 'em might come back to the house. I'm figurin' right now there's just one of 'em holding Texas."

"I'll go down there," Cass said. "You get over by the canyon rim. You can hold 'em off if they start back toward the house. Maybe if help comes, you'll get 'em in a crossfire."

"I'm not lettin' you do my job."

"Look, sheriff, I'm a lot younger'n you. I can move a lot faster, and I figure I'm better with a gun. You got your job to do back in Lost River with the vigilantes. I can't arrest them. You can."

"Whatta you mean, you're better with a gun?"

Cass grinned. "That's what I figure."

"Well, I admit you're a lot younger. You have a better chance, so go ahead. Now, that cabin's got one door. There's two front windows and one on the left side there. The back's got nothin' but rifle slots. But I don't know how you're gonna get inside.''

"They got a fire goin'. I'll try to plug the chimney.''

"Then good luck.''

They sat a long while on their heels, gazing at the valley far below. It was a certainty they were facing death. Within a few hours, they could both be history. After a moment, Cass reached out his hand to the sheriff, who took it firmly in his.

"I gotta say this,'' Cass said. "You're an ornery cuss, and mean as they come, but I ain't never met no lawman I respected more.''

"Well, you ain't no Sunday preacher, but I ain't never met a gunfighter I ever liked, afore now.''

Cass grinned. The lawman grimaced.

Then Cass, rifle in his right hand, rope in the other, began a slow descent with gloved hands. He was planning to make his way through the cattle and around the corrals and sheds. Some of the way, he would have to crawl on his belly. Once around the house, he would try to stuff the chimney with whatever was handy.

But if he wasn't careful, he would be a dead man. And Texas would be gone forever.

Chapter Ten

Moving behind the Poague's two-room house, covered with dirt and sore from his crawling through the valley, Cass took a moment to rest. It was midday and plenty warm. From the tack shed by the corrals, he had dragged a large pile of empty flour sacks. At the watering trough, he had soaked them briefly. Now he had to find a way to the roof.

Taking the rope he had carried with him, he drew a long loop. He prayed the sound would not be noticed. The chimney rose up from the center of the roof and was stone and narrow. Even if he couldn't stuff it, the sacks would drop and smother the fire, smoking them out.

Tossing the rope, he drew a deep breath as it circled and fell around the chimney. The sound was minimal. He put the sacks over his shoulders. Then he grabbed the length of the rope, his feet against the wall, and began to climb step by step, still wearing gloves.

It was tiring as he tried to be quiet. At last, he reached the roof and carefully crawled over to the chimney, dragging the sacks and being as quiet as possible. Now he rolled up the sacks in a big bundle and shoved them into the chimney. They took hold, blocking air.

He soon heard cussing inside as Rufus kicked at the fireplace. Gloves off, he moved on his belly across the roof. He lay flat with a view over the edge. He had his Colt in hand, waiting, a silent prayer for Texas on his lips.

Suddenly, Rufus came barreling out with his six-shooter drawn. Smoke poured out after him, but he kicked the door closed and stumbled forward, gasping for air.

Half drunk, Rufus stood out there for several minutes, exposed and staggering, looking around. Any moment he would realize someone was on the roof. Like now. He spun around and aimed upward, firing wildly.

Cass fired back, hitting him square between the eyes. The big man threw his arms up in frantic death, fell backward like timber and crashed to the ground in a huge mass. The earth seemed to shake under his body.

Cass swung down from the roof. At that moment, he heard gunfire from the far canyon. He turned to pull the door open. Smoke poured out, and he leaned inside, drawing his bandanna over his nose and mouth. He prayed Texas was there and alive.

As the smoke began to escape and clear, he saw her kneeling with a huge buffalo gun at her shoulder, the barrel resting on a chair, aimed at his middle. She was coughing. Her free hand continually sought to cover her nose.

Cass suddenly realized she didn't know it was him, and he jumped aside just as she fired. The rifle boomed like an explosion, the shot careening past his head. It knocked her over backward on the floor.

Frantic, she tried to grab spilled cartridges, but she was coughing badly, and Cass shouted.

"Hey, it's me!"

She tried to rise, but she was overcome by smoke and let the rifle slide from her grasp. She covered her face with both hands, still coughing and gasping for air.

Cass hurried over to her and took her hand, pulling her to her feet. She swayed, and he caught her up in his arms. She felt small and light as he dashed outside into the clear air. She was gasping for breath and clung to him even as he lowered her to the ground, kneeling at her side.

"Lie face down," he said.

She obeyed, and he pushed his hands down on her back several times while she continued to cough. Then he brought a bucket of water from the well. She turned over and sat up as he splashed her face, soaking her chemise. He gave her a scoop of water, and she drank hesitantly.

"I almost killed you," she said.

"You're lucky that old Sharps didn't blow up in your face."

She nodded with a half smile. "Yes, I could hardly see what I was doing."

Cass realized he was cold all over. Not because she had almost shot him, but because she had nearly died in there.

He turned to listen to the sudden, distant gunfire.

After a moment, Texas reached for his hand, her slim fingers in his strong grasp. He helped her stand. Still shaking, she moved against him, and his arm went slowly around her. The nearness of her, the worry and trauma he had just been through, all collected to drain him.

"Cass, Rufus killed your partner. He beat him with his rifle butt. And it was Rex that shot at you that day, killing Joker, trying to get you."

Abruptly, the gunfire in the distance came to a halt, leaving a dead silence. For a moment neither could speak, and then she pressed against him.

"Cass, I'm frightened."

"Maybe the sheriff got help."

But neither knew if it would be the Poagues or the law that came out of the pass. He released her and reloaded his sixgun. She picked up Rufus's weapon and shoved more cartridges inside the cylinder. He went back into the house and retrieved the old Sharps and some of the cartridges.

"What'll we do?" she asked.

"Fight it out from inside, now the smoke's gone."

"You were terribly brave."

"So were you."

She smiled up at him, and he grinned at her.

Now they waited. They saw dust, riders coming. He moved her around behind him, near the door, but she kept her hand on his right arm.

Soon, as the riders neared, they could see faces, and they were relieved. In front was the sheriff, who was leading Cass's stallion. Next to him rode Ross Langdon. Behind them were six of the rancher's hands and a dozen other angry men who loved Texas, including Swaps. There was no sign of the Poagues. Or Rick.

When the riders came to a halt in front of them, Ross was the first to speak. His square face was ashen. His handlebar mustache twitched as he looked from the dead Rufus to the girl at Cass' side.

"Thank the Lord you're all right, Texas."

"And the Poagues?" Cass asked.

The rancher leaned on the saddle horn. "The Poagues are all gone now. Back in the pass they was waitin' to ambush us, but the sheriff was up on the ridge behind 'em with his Winchester."

The sheriff looked around. "This place will go at auction. Might be all right, if it was kept up."

"No," said Ross. "Rufus had a wife, but he was right mean to her, so she went back to Ohio. My wife knows where. We'll send for her. Maybe some good will come of this.''

''Where's Rick?'' Cass asked, concerned about the jail.

''He wouldn't come,'' Ross said. ''Not that he wasn't thinkin' about you, Texas. He was worried about his brother.''

Webb frowned. ''We'd better get back.''

Cass mounted his stallion and with the sheriff, headed back toward the pass at a gallop, dust flying at their heels.

Texas took Ross's left arm and swung up behind him. She clung to him, her face against his heavy coat, tears in her eyes. As they rode, she held so tight, he felt her sob.

''Are you all right, Texas?'' he asked, turning his head.

''I have a problem, Mr. Langdon.''

''Who, that wild Cass Darringer?''

''I think I love him, but I can't let myself, because he just doesn't seem to feel anything for me.''

''I was a lot like him when I was his age, on both sides of the law now and then, wild as a wolf, with no eye for any woman. Then my wife came along, and I was nothin' but mush.''

''But I have no effect on him. Except a few kisses.''

''Trust me, Texas. Any kiss from you turned him

into jelly. If he lives through this, he's gonna come courtin', even if he don't know it yet. I promise.''

"If it ever happens, would you give me away?"

Ross sniffed back his tears and nodded.

It was a long way back to town. The only real danger there was Rick Langdon. But when Cass and the sheriff reached the jail at twilight, Myrtle was sitting on the desk, which was the makeshift wall, holding the shotgun. She was fully dressed with a heavy jacket.

Tully was perched next to her, eating a full meal from a tray. In the first cell was Rex, seated on his cot and glowering. In the second cell, the door tied with a chain, was Rick. Lumber and debris had been pushed aside and heaped up where the other outside wall had been.

Myrtle waved as the sheriff and Cass swung from the saddle and approached. She gave them a big smile. In fact, as she spoke, she looked right handsome. The pink lace at her throat, belying her black dress, made her look younger.

"It was like this, Sheriff. Tully here needed a couple minutes sleep, so I sat on watch. Next thing I know, here comes Rick. He tried to trick me, telling me he just wants to talk to his brother. Then he turns around and pulls his gun on poor Tully while he was sleeping.''

"So what happened?"

"So I hit him on the head with the shotgun.''

Tully was grinning as he downed his coffee. "You

shoulda seen it, sheriff. She knocked him down and took his gun away, all by herself. He looked up the barrel of her shotgun and started shakin' like jelly. Then I helped her lock 'im up. We got the chain there 'till you got back.''

Myrtle was pleased with herself. Webb stared at her with admiration, taking a second look at this hefty woman with the large brown eyes, wondering why he hadn't paid much attention to her. He took his keys and locked Rick's cell.

"Don't matter none," Rex called out. "You can't prove me or ole Rick was doin' anything at all."

The lawman explained what had happened out at the Poagues. "Texas is riding in with Ross Langdon and his men."

"Only three vigilantes left," Cass said. "The Poagues are dead. So are Jenks and Barnes. That leaves these two prisoners and Bixby."

"Bixby lit out," Tully said. "Packed his gear and left at sunup. Headin' south. But you can trail him easy enough. He's got that hammerhead roan with the big feet."

The sheriff and Cass turned to look at Myrtle as they realized what Cass had said about her husband. She was staring at them, eyes brimming.

"My husband would never—."

Rex laughed. "It's true, all right. Old Barnes wanted

to prove he was still a man, showing off the whole time. He even tied a noose."

Myrtle's eyes filled with tears, and she turned away, leaving them and heading up the street toward the rooming house in the twilight.

"I'm right sorry," Cass muttered.

"What about Bixby?" Tully asked.

"I'll go after him," Cass said. "At sunup."

Webb grimaced. "Only if I deputize you first. But remember, you're my best witness on Simmons's murder. And I can't hold up trial for long. But maybe you'd better take some men with you."

"Ranger would leave any horse behind. Besides, this is somethin' I gotta do. Until Bixby's caught, Shorty ain't gonna rest."

Webb pushed his hat back. "I heard once how Bixby's got a brother in Oregon he was braggin' about. I figure he'll turn west through the pass and along the Salmon River."

As they walked onto the boardwalk, they saw Ross Langdon, Texas behind his saddle, and the dozen riders entering town as dark shadows filled the street and the moon was rising. Cass stood watching as Ross reined up next to him. Gazing up at Texas, Cass couldn't help but reach for her. She leaned down. His hands caught her by the waist and lowered her as she smiled at him.

Cass reluctantly took his hands from Texas's waist when Myrtle came hurrying to embrace, then lead her away. Texas looked back over her shoulder to find Cass staring after her.

Later, Ross Langdon joined the sheriff and Cass for supper at Joe's Cafe.

"I don't know what to do," Ross said. "Texas told me Rex was plotting with Rufus to get rid of me so they could have my money and the ranch. A man makes a lot of mistakes in his life, but when his own sons turn on him, he's a failure."

Webb downed his coffee. "It was bad company."

"I can't use that excuse," Ross said. "Look at Cass. He ran off from home when he was a youngster, and afore long, he got tied up with the Red River gang. But he turned out all right."

Cass shrugged. "Thanks to Shorty. He never gave up on me."

"I can't help blamin' myself," Ross said. "Maybe if I had made my boys part owners, put their names on the deed like they wanted, they would have felt different."

"No," Webb said. "You woulda just made it easier for them. I figure they got on the wrong road a long time ago. And they did it all by themselves."

"Why didn't I see it?" the rancher asked.

"Maybe you did."

Ross wiped his eyes with the back of his hand, his body unsteady. They downed their coffee, and Ross went up to the hotel. After being deputized, Cass went to the rooming house for some sleep.

Before dawn, his gear packed, he found Bucky waiting downstairs. The boy followed him to the livery and stood back as Cass saddled and packed his stallion.

"Can I go with you, Cass?"

"No."

"Nothin's the same here anymore."

"It will be. Just give it time, Bucky. You have a good home."

"Mrs. Barnes, she says her husband was one of the vigilantes. She and Celia are up in their rooms, still cryin'. She wanted Celia to marry a Langdon so her husband could stop working, so he'd live longer, because he was so poorly. Now she figures it was all for nothin'."

"Everything will be all right, son."

Bucky smiled, sniffing. "You want me to be your son?"

"Well, uh, you got a home, Bucky. A good one. Now go take care of the women in your family."

"Maybe they want me all right, but don't a kid have a right to pick for hisself?"

"It sounds like the kid had better go to school."

Bucky looked sad and lost, and he turned away.

Cass mounted his stallion, heading southwest, finding Bixby's trail where he turned west toward the pass through the Bitterroot Mountains. For a week, he tracked the little man, finally cornering him inside a cluttered trading post along the Salmon River. When Bixby turned and saw him, he raised his rifle and pointed at Cass. The proprietor ducked behind his counter as Bixby snarled.

"Blast you, Darringer. What are you doin' here?"

"I've been lookin' for you."

"I knowed somebody was doggin' my trail."

"You're going back with me, Bixby. You're going to stand trial."

"We had a right to hang them fellas. We was sure they'd done it. They'd been flashin' new money right after the bank robbery. And the guard that was killed, he was a friend of everybody in town. We was all fired up."

"You didn't give 'em a chance to explain?"

"Oh, they was yellin' about workin' for the railroad, all right, but no one believed 'em. Only railroad we knowed was down in Salt Lake. Why that was near four hundred miles south. We figured they was lyin'."

"So you hanged 'em."

"We didn't know they was innocent 'till they was dead. Then Rufus rode along side 'em and started going through their pockets, lookin' for money. That's when we found out, and it was too late. So you gotta let me go."

"I'm taking you back."

Bixby's eyes narrowed, and he kept the rifle aimed at Cass's middle. Any second now.

Suddenly, Bixby pulled the trigger as Cass jumped aside, drew and fired, killing the man instantly. Bixby fell forward, then crumpled to the floor, face down.

Cass stood quiet a moment, staring down at the dead man and wondering if Shorty was watching. It was nearly over, and he didn't feel any better about it. Sadly, he left and headed back to the northwest.

Now that it was all winding down, he felt lost, alone. No it was worse. He was lonely, and he'd never felt that way before, not with Shorty around. Every night, he sat by the campfire, staring into the flames. At first he saw only the hanging and Shorty's body, and the faces of men he himself had shot down.

But as he neared Lost River, his last night on the trail was his most painful, because the face in the flames was Texas, gorgeous and smiling. He twirled his hat in his hands, thinking about her, knowing that when the trial was over, he was going to have to face himself. He wasn't sure he could ride away from her, but he couldn't believe she would ever want him, a gunfighter.

When he finally returned to Lost River, it had snowed but melted. The streets were muddy, a strong wind was blowing, and the sky was slate grey. He had a strange feeling of coming home. He reined up at the freight office and was distressed to see a closed sign. He dismounted and left his stallion tied at the railing.

He peered inside but saw no one, and he felt a worried twinge, until he saw other signs on other store fronts.

He walked through the mud to the jail with its new front wall and roof. He discovered it was the day of the trial. Three grim lawmen from Deer Lodge were seated near the stove. Sheriff Webb was at his desk, his beard trimmed, his clothes cleaned, and looking like he had just had a bath.

Myrtle was there and had just brought the sheriff a large chocolate cake which he was cutting into with delight. She wasn't wearing black anymore, except for her shawl.

"We waited as long as we could," the sheriff said to Cass. "Did you get Bixby?"

"I had to cut him down."

Rex and Rick were gripping the bars, glaring at Cass as he returned his badge to the desk.

"So you got Bixby," Rex said. "Well, he was the only one left what knew anything about a hanging. So you got nothin', sheriff. It's our word against yours and Jenks, and he's dead."

The lawman tasted the cake. He ate a big chunk of it. He looked as happy as a gruff man could be. Myrtle smiled, and he winked at her. With a giggle like a school girl's, she turned and hurried out of the jail.

Cass grinned. "So that's how the wind blows."

"Don't knock it, son. That's a fine woman. And I'm gettin' too old to be lookin' after myself."

At that moment, the door opened again. Tully entered. He was clean, fresh shaven and wearing a deputy's badge. He reached out and seized Cass's hand, shaking it with vigor. He looked like a happy man.

"Speakin' of romance," said the sheriff, "just take a look at what it's done to Tully. He and Celia Barnes been sparkin' every day of the week, now that I got her mother straightened out."

Tully grinned from ear to ear. "Well, we figure we're gonna have a weddin' right soon, now that I'm gonna be foreman out at the Lost River ranch. Mr. Langdon's even buildin' us a house. I'm doin' all right for a second hand cowboy."

Cass stood looking at both men with envy, but his past lay heavy on his heart, and his Colt felt like a ton hanging low on his hip.

"But Cass, you'd better watch out," Tully said. "Old Krutz, he's got his son pantin' after Texas and all her money."

Immediately, Cass flushed with anger and jealousy.

He looked for Texas as he watched the lawmen move the prisoners down to the town hall, which was set up as a courthouse with chairs and benches, and he looked for her in the crowd, unable to find that flame-red hair.

The judge was a greying, scholarly-looking man with a distinguished manner. When he sat behind the desk, it somehow magically transformed itself into a high bench of justice. Everyone behaved accordingly.

The prisoners were placed at a table to the judge's right. Their lawyer was banker Krutz, who professed to some knowledge and experience in law. Sheriff Webb was prosecuting as there was no one else who qualified.

"Your Honor," the lawman said, "Rex Langdon and Rick Langdon are both charged with conspiracy and the murders of three men who were hanged by vigilantes and accessories to the murder of one Shorty Greene. Rick Langdon is also charged with the attempted murder of Deputy Tully. Rex Langdon is charged with the murder of Mr. Simmons, Joker Rafferty and the attempted murder of Cass Darringer."

Rex leaned over to Rick and whispered. "Ain't no way they're gonna convict us. All them witnesses are dead. We just gotta keep our mouths shut."

Chapter Eleven

Cass was up front but couldn't concentrate on the proceedings. He kept looking around for Texas. He finally saw Celia and Myrtle in the back row of the crowded room. And there was Ross Langdon, head down.

When Sheriff Webb testified about the dying declaration of Jenks, Cass had to do the questioning. Over Krutz's constant objections, everything Jenks had confessed was told.

Then Cass testified to Rex's murder of Simmons. Krutz came on strong with a cross-examination, trying to discredit Cass.

"Isn't it true that it was you who killed Simmons?"

"No."

"Isn't it true you blamed the vigilantes for your partner's murder and believed Rex and Rick Langdon to have been among them?"

"Yes."

"Isn't killing your profession?"

Webb called out. "Objection."

"Your honor," Krutz said, "Mr. Darringer's reputation is well known. I have a right to attack his veracity.''

The judge overruled the objection. Krutz smiled.

''Now then, Mr. Darringer, isn't killing your profession?''

''No.''

''How many men have you killed in gunfights?''

''Maybe twelve.''

''You are so disdainful that you don't even keep count?''

The sheriff objected and was sustained, and in redirecting the question, Webb asked Cass about the men he had killed.

''I never killed a man who didn't try to kill me first.''

But Krutz was still satisfied that Cass was painted as a man blind with revenge.

Texas was called and came inside the building on the arm of a tall handsome young stranger in a grey suit. Wearing a yellow dress with lace at the throat, she looked unbearably beautiful. Cass was so glad to see her, he was beside himself. He agonized over seeing her with someone else, and he figured this was the banker's son. Fiercely jealous, he felt his face burning hot.

With Texas on the stand, Sheriff Webb laid the foundation, leading her testimony from the abduction to the ranch. ''And then Rufus Poague took you to his cabin?''

"Yes. He said his cousins would ambush you and Mr. Darringer when you came through the pass."

"What else did he tell you?"

"That once you and Mr. Darringer were dead, he would get Rex out of jail."

Over Krutz's objections, she related how Rufus and his kin worked with Rex and Rick to rustle Langdon cattle. She told how Rufus confessed to the hanging, to killing Shorty and taking the horses to Rex and Rick.

"He said they split the money. And then he said that Rex wanted to do away with his own father. And that Rex had killed Joker."

Krutz continued to object, calling the testimony hearsay, and was constantly overruled. The judge was getting annoyed and pounded his gavel, then leaned forward and spoke with a heavy voice.

"Mr. Poague is not available to testify, and his statements were admissions of guilt. Now would counsel let the witness finish her story without interruption?"

Krutz was red-faced. Rex and Rick Langdon were frantic. Seated with their hands cuffed behind them, they looked doomed. Upon cross-examination, Krutz knew he had to shake Texas's testimony by first attacking her credibility.

Yet she was his richest depositor, and Krutz had big personal plans for that money. With great difficulty, he proceeded, avoiding any direct attack.

"Miss Texas, isn't it true that Cass Darringer told you what to say?"

"No."

"Aren't you in love with him?"

She flushed. "I don't know."

"And isn't it true that Cass Darringer asked you to marry him?"

"No."

Frustrated, Krutz gave up. The sheriff asked her only one question. "Miss Texas, prior to the time you received your fortune, had any man in this valley asked you to be his wife?"

"Yes. Rex Langdon."

"And your answer?"

"I told him I'd think about it."

The alleged bias had been turned around. Krutz was again frustrated. He sat grimly through Swaps's credible testimony, then attacked him without success. When all of the witnesses had testified, Krutz knew they were in trouble. In desperation, he called Rex to the stand.

"All lies," Rex said, to every recall of testimony.

"Where were you the day of the alleged lynching?"

"Me and Rick were out huntin' strays in the ridges up behind Sweet Meadow. But anything at all happens around here, we get blamed."

"And were you behind the dancehall the night of Mr. Simmons's murder?"

"Why, sure. I come around there and caught Darringer beating my friend Simmons. I aimed my rifle at Darringer. That's when Swaps came out and saw us. And Darringer said it was me that done it."

During cross-examination, Rex couldn't be shaken. He was a credible witness. The jury was confused, and when the court adjourned temporarily, they retired to the back room.

Everyone filed back outside except the prisoners, Sheriff Webb, his deputy and the three lawmen from Deer Lodge. The crowd was left with the feeling that the Langdon boys could well get off free and clear.

In the sunlight, Ross Langdon looked pale and the whites of his eyes were red. He joined some of his men across the street and sat in the shade, staring at his boots.

Myrtle and Celia stood with a group of women in the shade near the rooming house. Cass wandered into the street with the crowd, not knowing where to go, until he saw Texas and the fancy stranger who kept dusting off his fancy suit, giving Cass the urge to run over and kick dirt on him. Sometimes, the man would run his fingers over his slicked blond hair. Texas saw Cass and waved him over to them.

Cass strolled over, jealousy eating him inside out. The man was exactly Cass's height so they could look directly at each other. Texas sensed the hostility but smiled.

"Cass Darringer, this is Jon Krutz. He's new in town. His father owns the bank."

Cass grimly shook the man's hand. His imagination running wild, he figured that Krutz, finding himself with an account that belonged to a rich, single young woman, had made a lot of plans for his son. Cass told himself he had to protect Texas from this farce before he left town.

"I'm glad you're back safely," she said to Cass. "Did you find Mr. Bixby?"

He tried to read what was in her eyes. "I had to kill him."

Jon Krutz made a face. "I suppose that was easy for a gunfighter."

"It's never easy. What's your line of work?"

"Banking, of course. A most respected profession. One that allows a man to have a wife and family."

"I've known bankers who've run off with the money."

The two men glared at each other. Texas, who was much shorter than them, was unable to block their views. She tried standing taller but they refused to look down at her. Jon was so arrogant, Cass wanted to flatten his nose.

"Cass, do you think Rex will be convicted?" she asked.

"Hard to say. There are no live witnesses to the hanging and Shorty's murder. And Swaps didn't see

Rex hit Simmons. And weren't no blood on the butt of Rex's rifle. Our testimony seemed slanted. And Rex was a good witness for himself. It could go either way.''

Someone called out that the jury had reached a verdict. Jon Krutz dusted his suit off carefully. Then he took Texas's arm and put it through his. She reached out with her other hand and took Cass's arm.

Cass walked with them, but he was getting angrier by the minute. This was no man for Texas. He'd have to explain that to her, before he left town.

Back inside and seated, the crowd waited as the twelve men returned. The foreman stood up with his beard twitching as he read from the piece of paper in his hairy hand.

"Your honor, we found Rex Langdon and Rick Langdon guilty on all counts."

The crowd erupted in chatter, forcing the judge to silence them with his gavel. Rex was shaking all over, and Rick was bowing his head. Both men slumped in their seats. Banker Krutz nearly collapsed himself.

The judge cleared his throat. "Now then, will the prisoners rise?"

The judge's voice hung heavy in the room as he spoke in a calm, serious tone. He sentenced Rick to twenty years in the Territorial Prison at Deer Lodge, citing Rex's influence on the younger brother. He sentenced Rex to life at Deer Lodge with no possibility of parole.

The prisoners were so badly shaken, they nearly fell back into their chairs, but Rex felt his neck with the realization he wasn't going to hang.

The prisoners were taken by the Deer Lodge lawmen and herded out the back way. As Cass walked out the front, looking for Texas, he saw Ross Langdon tightening the cinch on his saddle. The rancher had no color, and his eyes were wet, downcast, as Cass approached.

"Mr. Langdon, I'm right sorry."

"I reckon you are. This will be mighty hard on their mother. As soon as I see my boys once more, I gotta ride out and break the news. At least Rex ain't gonna hang, and maybe we'll get Rick back someday. But you ain't to blame, Cass. I'd have done the same as you, under the circumstances."

Cass stood back as the rancher mounted. Then Ross Langdon leaned forward on the pommel and looked down at him.

"I'd take it kindly if you'd visit me now and then. Maybe we could go huntin'."

"I'd like that."

"You maybe oughta settle here, over at Sweet Meadow. I reckon I don't need every blade o' grass, and I want you to have it. I'll help you get started with some stock, and my men can help you build."

"There's no need."

"It's the way I want it."

"Thanks, Mr. Langdon."

"And bring Texas around when you come. I like that girl. Visits my wife and makes her sit up and get around some. Doc was out yesterday and said my wife is gonna live a long time after all. I think she figures she's got herself a daughter. And I wouldn't mind havin' me a son I could be proud of."

Ross reached down with an outstretched hand. Cass, a huge lump in his throat, took it in a firm shake. Then the rancher turned and rode down toward the jail. Cass stared after him with a racing heart. The rancher had made it obvious they could be friends, good friends. Like father and son.

Cass swallowed hard and turned around, looking for Texas. She was walking with Jon Krutz and came to take Cass's arm, leading them toward the freight office.

"I'm going to show Mr. Krutz my new investment. It's in our corral, out back."

Cass, figuring she had bought herself a riding horse or a buggy outfit, nodded and walked to her left while Jon Krutz hovered to her right, ignoring Cass.

"Some trial," said Jon. "My father did very well, just the same. He's a brilliant man. It runs in the family."

Texas nodded. "I admit he could have been harder on me. But I could tell he doesn't like business women."

"But you'll be giving that up, won't you?" Jon asked.

Texas nodded. "I may sell out."

"You have to start a new life. I want to help you."

When it was time to cross the muddy street, Jon Krutz removed his small brimmed hat and turned politely to Texas, but he was too late. Cass had swept her up in his arms, and she didn't seem to mind.

As they crossed, his stallion, tied in front of the freight office, tossed its head and pawed at the mud.

At the back corrals, Texas pointed to the enclosure where Bucky was sitting on the top rail. There were seven mares. One of them was the pinto mare that Cass and Shorty had trapped. The other six were fine sorrels and bays with good lines. She pressed to the fence, her back to the men.

"All seven?" Jon asked, making a face. "Texas, you really do need a man to handle your affairs. This was a foolish purchase. Now one, I can see, if you must ride. But what will you ever do with seven mares?"

"Why, raise colts and fillies," she said.

"You need a stallion for that."

She turned slowly, smiling at Cass. "I know where there's a fine buckskin stallion."

"What's going on here?" Jon demanded.

Cass's heart was pounding like crazy. Texas was smiling at him with her entire soul glistening in her blue eyes. The sun danced on her hair, and she looked intensely beautiful.

"Texas, let's go over to the bank," Jon said, clearly annoyed. "I was going to suggest some real investments."

She shook her head. "No, I'm sorry, Jon. Please go on without me. I have to make plans."

"Plans? What plans? Stay away from this man. He's a gunfighter. You can't trust him."

It was then that Bucky came down from the railing and stood between her and Jon, trying to look big as he spoke.

"Mr. Darringer is not a gunfighter. He's my friend."

"Get outta the way," Jon snapped, shoving the boy aside and behind him.

Bucky nearly fell on the wet manure pile where flies were thick. He recovered his balance and backed away.

Angered, Cass moved forward, his hand on his holster. "I'm thinkin' it's time you just moved on, Krutz."

"I'm not afraid of you, Darringer."

Cass took a step forward. Texas moved aside. Strangely enough, the dandy peeled off his fancy coat and loosened his little tie. He handed his coat to Texas, smoothed his hair and smiled.

Then Jon took a stance, knees bent outward, feet pointed the same way. He positioned his fists, his right held high. He looked like a rooster.

"Ever do bare knuckle fighting, Darringer? I was college champion. This face was never touched. So come on, let's see how much you can take."

Cass walked right up to him and rammed his fist in the man's face so fast, Jon didn't see it coming. Jon was stunned by the blow, staggering backward, shaking his head, blood trickling from his nose. He was furious but calm.

"You don't know the rules, Darringer. Just do what I do."

Again Jon took his stance. Then he danced a little forward, trying to impress Texas. He jabbed at the air, smiling his arrogance.

Cass moved in suddenly and hammered his fist in the man's face. This time, Jon was so stunned his eyes went blank. Cass hit him again on the jaw. Jon staggered backward, losing his balance and sitting hard on the wet pile of fresh manure, scattering the flies. There was blood on his mouth.

Cass's right hand was cut raw. He stood quiet, waiting.

Shaking his head, his brain rattled, Jon felt the wet stink under his seat. With a gasp, he managed to get to his feet and brushed at his rear. He could barely stand and was red-faced. He took his coat from Texas and draped it over his shoulder.

"You're no gentleman, Darringer. I can't fight a savage. Are you coming, Miss Texas?"

She shook her head. Angry, frustrated, Jon turned away, storming off toward the street, his shoulders squared. The seat of his pants was one big wet splotch.

Texas put her hand to her lips to try to stop a giggle, but it was too late. Cass, still sweating and breathing hard, stared at her with delight.

She put her slim fingers on his arm. "We'll have wonderful children. And a new start in life."

Children? Marriage? Cass Darringer? His mouth was so dry, he couldn't respond right away. Her words reminded him she knew all about the life he had led and well understood. He thought of Shorty, now avenged and resting in peace, leaving Cass with no place to go.

And he thought of Langdon's offer. He could see a little house on the hill at Sweet Meadow. There would be a picket fence. It wouldn't keep out the deer, but it would be pretty.

There would be corrals, barns, colts and fillies. And children. Lots of happy kids, wanted and needed. He would go hunting with Ross Langdon, maybe for days at a time, sitting around the campfire together in the wilderness. He wanted it all, badly.

Yet all he could do was stare at her.

"Cass, don't you want to marry me?"

It was then that Bucky, gazing from one to the other, turned and walked toward the street, out of earshot, pausing at the back corner of the freight office to kick at some rocks. His head was bowed to one side. His small hand picked up a stone.

Cass watched the lonely orphan as his own mind clicked. It clicked so fast, words fell out of his mouth.

"Texas, I'm no bargain, but if you'll take the both of us, me and the boy, maybe you wouldn't be sorry."

She didn't hesitate and called out. "Bucky, wait."

The boy turned and looked back. She held out her hand. He came slowly toward them, not knowing what she wanted. He stopped some ten feet away, playing with the small stone in his hands.

"Bucky, Mr. Darringer and I want you to be our first son."

Bucky stared. His blue eyes were wide open, freckles red in the sun. Then suddenly, he threw the rock away and rushed to her and threw his arms around her, his face at her waist, hugging her so tight, she couldn't move.

Cass had a strange feeling of elation, of being born for the first time. All of his past misery and anger just faded away. His slate was suddenly clean, and when Bucky turned to him, the joy in the boy's eyes was near unbearable to see.

"Oh, boy!" He looked up with a grin they would never forget. "You really mean it?"

"Yes," she said. "We want you with us, Bucky."

"Wow. I got me a real home."

He hugged Cass as high as he could reach, all three

with tears in their eyes. Then Bucky wrapped his arms around her again and wouldn't let go for a long moment. Then he backed away with a grin.

"I gotta go tell the sheriff and Tully. But don't you go anywhere without me."

"Don't worry," Cass said. "We're stuck with each other."

Bucky jumped around, hugged himself, and ran for the street, while they stared after him and sniffed back their tears. Before he disappeared, he paused to jump up and down and wave, and they waved back.

They could hear Cass's stallion nickering from the railing in front of the office. The suddenly restless mares began moving around the corral. The pinto tossed its head and mane, then ran around the enclosure and bucked.

Time was awasting.

Texas moved into his arms. "I loved you at first sight, Cass Darringer, but you haven't said you loved me."

"Reckon I do, but I didn't know it for sure until that fool Jon put his hands on you."

"You sure took care of him."

He grinned. "Yeah, I sure did. The flies was followin' him all the way down the street."

Texas smiled, eyes sparkling, as she nestled close.

Cass was overwhelmed by his blessings. Shorty had saved him from the outlaw trail and had been avenged,

Ross Langdon wanted Cass for a son, Bucky wanted him for a father, and the prettiest woman in the territory loved him.

As his lips found hers in a gentle, searching kiss, his fingers deep in her silken red hair, he realized he had spent his life heading for Lost River and this woman's arms.

Cass Darringer had found the end of his trail.